Madison Entered The Dining Room

wearing a slim black skirt that came right above her knees, conservative heels and a simple white blouse. But Sheikh Zain knew better. That professional, prim and proper persona only served to conceal the daring beneath her cool exterior. He'd wager his kingdom that she had on a pair of brightly colored panties.

A richly detailed fantasy assaulted him, one that involved sitting beside her and running his hand up the inside of her thigh and—

"Where would you like me?"

He thought of several answers, none of them appropriate. "Are you referring to the seating arrangements, or do you have something else in mind?"

Dear Reader,

Throughout my thirteen-year career, I've often been asked: What exactly is a "sheikh" book, and why do they have such widespread popularity? I can't speak for every author who's ventured into the realm of the sheikh mystique or every reader who is drawn to it. But I can address what I consider every time I write one of my own—give the story a relatable, modern twist while maintaining the fantasy.

Fantasy is definitely the key. Who doesn't want to escape to an exotic, magical locale in a fictional faraway land? And, let's face it, there's nothing more alluring than a dark, mysterious and, of course, gorgeous hero who possesses untold riches as well as a wealth of honor. Although this Arabian prince might be steeped in tradition, those very traditions oftentimes create serious conflict when he encounters a woman who is deemed anything but suitable. Yet from the moment he sees that woman, he's initially driven by lust and determined to reject anything other than a temporary liaison.

Enter a strong, independent heroine capable of bringing him to his emotional knees without really trying. Of course, she is completely drawn into his sensual lair by his touch and by the whispered words she doesn't necessarily understand, but the message comes through loud and clear. The chemistry is explosive, control goes out the window, the sexual tug and pull is ever present, and the emotional entanglement can only lead to disaster when it comes to differing cultures. But anything's possible when it involves that universal thing called love, and that is the basis for every satisfying romance.

I now invite you to enter Bajul, an ancient, diverse country that has been ruled for many years by the Mehdi family. The newest generation has now burst onto the scene, beginning with Sheikh Zain Mehdi, who's out to prove he is the best king for the job despite his lengthy absence. Trouble is, he finds it very hard to concentrate on his duties when Madison Foster enters his world. He's determined not to fail and definitely not to fall for her. Too bad the best-laid plans go awry.

Happy reading, and here's wishing you a very satisfying Arabian fantasy!

Kristi

KRISTI GOLD

THE RETURN OF THE SHEIKH

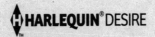

Recycling programs
for this product may
not exist in your area.

ISBN-13: 978-0-373-73243-2

THE RETURN OF THE SHEIKH

Copyright © 2013 by Kristi Goldberg

Printed in U.S.A.

www.Harlequin.com

___

KRISTI GOLD

has a fondness for beaches, baseball and bridal reality shows. She firmly believes that love has remarkable, healing powers and feels very fortunate to be able to weave stories of love and commitment. As a bestselling author, a National Readers' Choice Award winner and a Romance Writers of America three-time RITA® Award finalist, Kristi has learned that although accolades are wonderful, the most cherished rewards come from networking with readers. She can be reached through her website at www.kristigold.com or through Facebook.

To all the readers who continue to
embrace the romance genre through your belief
that love has the power to conquer all.
You are appreciated more than you know.

One

The moment Madison Foster exited the black stretch limo, a security detail converged upon her, signaling the extreme importance of her prospective client. The light mist turned to rain as she crossed the parking lot. One massive guard was on her right, a somewhat smaller man at her left, while two other imposing goons dressed in dark suits led the way toward the Los Angeles high-rise. A few feet from the service entrance, she heard a series of shouts and camera shutters, but she didn't dare look back. Making that fatal error could land her on the cover of some seedy tabloid with a headline that read The Playboy Prince's Latest Paramour. And a disheveled presumed paramour at that. She could already feel the effects of the humidity on her unruly hair as curls began to form at her nape beneath the low ponytail. So much for the sleek, professional look. So much for the farce that it never rained in sunny Southern California.

When the guards opened the heavy metal door and ushered her inside, Madison stepped carefully onto the damp tile surface as if walking on black ice. Couldn't they see she was wearing three-inch heels? Clearly they didn't care, she realized as they navigated the mazelike hallway at a rapid clip. Fortunately they guided her into a carpeted corridor before she took a tumble and wounded her pride, or worse. They soon reached a secluded elevator at the end of the passage where one man keyed in a code on the pad next to the door.

Like a well-oiled human machine, they moved inside the car. Madison felt as if she were surrounded by a contingent of stoic man-crows. They kept their eyes trained straight ahead, not one affording her even a casual glance, much less a kind word, on the trip to the top floor.

The elevator came to a smooth stop a few moments later where the doors slid open to a gentleman dressed in a gray silk suit, his sparse scalp and wire-rimmed glasses giving him a somewhat scholarly appearance. As soon as Madison exited the car, he offered his hand and a hesitant smile. "Welcome, Miss Foster. I'm Mr. Deeb, His Highness's personal assistant."

Madison wasn't pleased with the "Miss" reference, but for the sake of decorum, she shook his hand and returned his smile without issuing a protest. "It's nice to meet you, Mr. Deeb."

"And I you." He then stepped aside and made a sweeping gesture to his right. "Come with me, please."

With the guards bringing up the rear like good little soldiers, they traveled down the penthouse's black marble vestibule beneath soaring, two-story ceilings. As a diplomat's daughter and political consultant, she'd been exposed to her share of opulence, but she wasn't so jaded she couldn't appreciate good taste. A bank of tall windows revealing the Hollywood Hills drew her attention before her focus fell on the polished steel staircase winding upward to the second story. The clean lines and contemporary furnishings were straight out of a designer's dream, but not at all what she'd expected. She'd envisioned jewels and gold and statues befitting of royalty, not a bachelor pad. An extremely wealthy bachelor's pad nonetheless. Only the best would do for Sheikh Zain ibn Aahil Jamar Mehdi, the crown prince of Bajul, who'd recently and unexpectedly become the imminent king, the reason why she'd been summoned—to restore the tarnished reputation of the man with many names. In less than a month.

After they passed beneath the staircase and took an immediate right, Madison regarded Mr. Deeb, who also seemed bent on sprinting to the finish line. "I'm surprised the prince was willing to meet with me this late in the evening."

Deeb tugged at his tie but failed to look at her. "Prince Rafiq determined the time."

Rafiq Mehdi, Prince Zain's brother, had been the one who'd hired her, so that made sense. Yet she found Deeb's odd demeanor somewhat disturbing. "His Highness is expecting me, isn't he?"

They stopped before double mahogany doors at the end of the hall where Deeb turned to face her. "When Prince Rafiq called to say you were coming, I assumed he had spoken to his brother about the matter, but I am not certain."

If Rafiq hadn't told his brother about the plan, Madison could be tossed out before her damp clothes had time to dry. "Then you're not sure if he even knows I'm here, much less why I'm here?"

Blatantly ignoring Madison's question, Deeb pointed to a small alcove containing two peacock-patterned club chairs. "If you wish to be seated, I will come for you when the emir is prepared to see you."

Provided the man actually decided to see her.

After the assistant executed an about-face and disappeared through the doors, Madison claimed a chair, smoothed a palm over her navy pencil skirt and prepared to wait. She surveyed the guards lined up along the walls with two positioned on either side of the entry. Heavily armed guards. Not surprising. When a soon-to-be-king was involved, enemies were sure to follow. She'd initially been considered a possible threat, apparent when they rifled through her leather purse looking for concealed weapons before she'd entered the limo. She highly doubted she could do much damage with a tube of lipstick and a nail file.

Madison suddenly detected the sound of a raised voice, though she couldn't make out what that voice might be saying. Even if she could, she probably wouldn't understand most of the Arabic words. Yet there was no mistaking someone was angry, and she'd bet her last bottle of merlot she knew the identity of that someone.

Zain Mehdi reportedly didn't know the meaning of restraint, evidenced by his questionable activities. The notorious sheikh had left his country some seven years ago and taken up residence in the States. He'd often disappeared for months at a time, only to surface with some starlet or supermodel on his arm, earning him the title "Phantom Prince of Arabia."

That behavior hadn't necessarily shocked Madison. Many years ago, she'd met him at a dinner party she'd attended with her parents in Milan. Back then, he'd been an incurable sixteen-year-old flirt. Not that he'd flirted with her, or that he would even remember her at all, a gawky preteen with no confidence. A girl who'd been content to blend into the background, very much like her mother.

She didn't do the blending-in thing these days. She intended to be front and center, and if she managed to succeed at this assignment, that would prove to be another huge feather in her professional cap.

When the doors opened wide, Madison came to her feet, adjusted her white linen jacket and held her breath in hopes that she wouldn't be dismissed. "Well?" she asked when Deeb didn't immediately speak.

"The emir will see you now," he said, his tone somewhat wary. "But he is not happy about it."

As long as she had the opportunity to win him over, Madison didn't give a horse's patoot about the prince's current mood. "Fair enough."

Deeb opened the door and followed her inside the well-appointed office. But she didn't have the time—or the inclination—to study the room further. The six-foot-plus man leaning back against the massive desk, arms folded across his chest, his intense gaze contrasting with his casual stance, now captured her complete attention. Publicity photos—or her distant memories—definitely didn't do Zain Mehdi justice.

With his perfectly symmetrical features, golden skin and deep brown eyes framed by ridiculously long black lashes, he could easily be pegged as a Hollywood star preparing to play the role of a Middle Eastern monarch. Yet he'd forgone the royal robes for a white tailored shirt rolled up at the sleeves and a pair of dark slacks. He also wore an expression that said he viewed her as an intruder.

Madison tamped down her nerves, shored up her

frame and faked a calm facade. "Good evening, Your Highness. I'm Madison Foster."

He studied her offered hand but ignored the gesture. "I know who you are. You are the daughter of Anson Foster, a member of the diplomatic corps and a longtime acquaintance of my father's."

At least he remembered her father, even if he probably didn't remember her. "My sincerest condolences on your loss, Your Highness. I'm sure the king's sudden passing came as quite a shock."

He shifted his weight slightly, a sure sign of discomfort. "Not as shocking as learning of his death two weeks after the fact."

"The emir was traveling when his father passed," Deeb added from behind Madison.

The sheikh sent his assistant a quelling look. "That will be all, Deeb. Ms. Foster and I will continue this conversation in private."

Madison glanced over her shoulder to see Deeb nodding before he said, "As you wish, Emir."

As soon as the right-hand man left the room, the sheikh strolled around the desk, dropped down into the leather chair and gestured toward the opposing chair. "Be seated."

Say please, Madison wanted to toss out. Instead, she slid into the chair, set her bag at her feet and made a mental note to work on his manners. "Now that we've established you know who I am, do you understand why I'm here?"

He leaned back and streaked a palm over his shadowed jaw. "You are here at my brother's request, not mine. According to Rafiq, you are one of the best political consultants in this country. *If* your reputation holds true."

If his reputation held true, she had her work cut out for her. "I've worked alongside political strategists in successfully assisting high-profile figures with public perception."

"And why do you believe I would need your assistance with that?"

Okay, she'd draw him a picture, but it wouldn't be pretty. "For starters, you haven't been back to Bajul in years. Second, I know there's concern that you won't be welcomed with open arms when you do return to assume your position as king. And last, there is the issue with the women."

He had the gall to give her a devil-may-care grin. "You cannot believe everything you hear, Ms. Foster."

"True, but many people believe what they read. Therefore, it's imperative we convey that you're focused on being an effective leader like your father."

His smile disappeared out of sight. "Then I am to assume you wish to mold me into the image of my father."

She found the comment to be extremely telling. "No. I want to help you build a more favorable image of yourself."

"And how do you propose to do that?"

Very carefully. "By reintroducing you to your people through a series of public appearances and social events."

He inclined his head and studied her straight-on. "You intend to invite the entire country to a cocktail party?"

She could now add *sarcastic* along with *sexy* to his list of attributes. "The social events would be private. I'll include only those in your close circle of friends and your family, as well as members of the governing council. Possibly a few foreign dignitaries and politicians and perhaps some investors."

He grabbed a pen from the desktop and began to turn it over and over. "Go on."

At least he seemed mildly interested. "As far as the public appearances are concerned, I have a lot of experience with speech writing," she said. "I'd be happy to assist you with that."

He frowned. "I have a graduate degree in economics from Oxford and I am fluent in five languages, Ms. Foster. What makes you think I cannot compose my own speeches in an articulate manner?"

Nothing like stepping on his royal pride. "I'm sure you're quite capable, Your Highness, which is why I said I'd *assist* you. What you say and how you say it will be extremely important in winning over the masses."

He tossed the pen aside and released a gruff sigh. "I have no reason to engage in political maneuvering. In the event you haven't heard, my position is already secure. I was chosen to be king, and my word is the law. I *am* the law."

"True, but when people are happy with their leader, that makes for a more peaceful country. And we have less than a month before your official coronation to change your country's opinion of you. During that time, we'll cover all the details, from the way you speak and act to the way you dress."

He sent her a sly, overtly sensual smile. "Will you be dressing me?"

The sudden images flitting around Madison's mind would be deemed less than appropriate. They even leaned a little toward being downright dirty. "I'm sure your staff can assist you with that."

"It's unfortunate that's not among your duties," he said. "I would be more inclined to agree to your plan."

As far as she was concerned, he could put that charisma card right back into the deck. "Look, I realize you're used to charming women into doing your bidding, but that tact doesn't work with me."

He gave her a skeptical look. "If I decide to accept your offer, would you be willing to stay on after the coronation?"

She hadn't expected that question. "Possibly, if you could afford to keep me on staff. My services aren't cheap."

He released a sharp, cynical laugh. "Look around, Ms. Foster. Does it appear I'm destitute?"

Not even close. "We can discuss the possibility later. Right now, we need to concentrate on the current issue at hand, if you're willing to work with me."

He studied the ceiling for a moment before bringing his gaze back to hers. "The answer is no, I am not willing to work with you. I am quite capable of handling my own affairs."

She wasn't ready to give up without pointing out the most major concern. "Speaking of affairs, I'm also skilled when it comes to dealing with scandals, in case you have any of those little sex skeletons hiding in a closet."

His expression turned steely as he stood. "My apologies for wasting your time, but I believe we are finished now."

Apparently she'd hit a serious nerve, and yes, they were definitely finished.

Madison came to her feet, withdrew a business card from her bag and placed it on the desk. "Should you change your mind, here's my number. I'll let you break the news to your brother."

"Believe me, I have much to stay to my brother," he said. "That is first on my agenda when I return to Bajul."

She'd like to have front row seats to that. She'd also like to think he might reconsider. Unfortunately, neither fell into the realm of possibility at the moment. "I wish you all the best for a smooth transition, Your Highness. Again, let me know if you decide you need my services."

After slipping the bag's strap back on her shoulder, Madison covered her disappointment with a determined walk to the door. But before she made a hasty exit, the sheikh called her back. "Yes?" she said as she faced him, trying hard not to seem too hopeful.

He'd rounded the desk and now stood only a few feet away. "You've changed quite a bit since we first met all those years ago."

The fact he did recall the dinner party, and he hadn't bothered to mention it before now, thoroughly shocked her. "I'm surprised you remember me at all."

"Very difficult to forget such an innocent face, ocean-blue eyes and those remarkable blond curls."

Here came the annoying blush, right on cue. "I wore glasses and braces and my hair was completely out of control." Which had all been remedied with laser eye surgery, orthodontists and flat irons.

He took a few steps toward her. "You wore a pink dress, and you were very shy. You barely glanced my way."

Oh, but she had. Several times. When he hadn't been looking. "I've since gotten over the shyness."

"I noticed that immediately. I've also noticed you've grown into a very beautiful woman."

Madison barely noticed anything but his dark, pensive eyes when he walked right up to her, leaving little space between them. "Now that we've established my transformation," she said, "I need to get to the airport so I don't miss my flight to D.C." She needed to get away from him before his extreme magnetism commandeered her common sense.

"I do have a private jet," he said, his gaze unwavering. "You are welcome to use it whenever it is available. If you plan to travel to the region in the future, feel free to contact me and I'll arrange to have you transported to Bajul. I would enjoy having you as my guest. I could show you things you've never seen before. Give you an experience you will not easily forget."

She'd enjoy being his guest, perhaps too much. "You mean an evening trek by camel, or perhaps on the back of an elephant, across the desert? You'll feed me pomegranates while we're entertained by dancing girls?"

He looked more amused than offended by her cynicism. "I prefer all-terrain vehicles to camels and pachyderms, I detest pomegranates, but dancing would be an option. Between us, of course."

She didn't dare dance with him, much less take a midnight ride with him in any form or fashion. "As fascinating as that sounds, and as much as I appreciate the offer, I won't be traveling outside the U.S. now that I won't be working with you. But thank you for the invitation, and have a safe trip home."

This time when Madison hurried away, the future king closed the doors behind her, a strong reminder that another important career door had closed.

However, she refused to give in to defeat. Not quite yet. As soon as the sheikh returned home, he might decide he needed her after all.

He greatly needed an escape.

The absolute loss of freedom weighed heavily on Zain as the armored car navigated the steep drive leading to the palace. So did the less-than-friendly reception. A multitude of citizens lined the drive, held back by the guards charged with his protection. Some had their fists raised in anger, others simply scowled. Because of the bulletproof glass, he couldn't quite make out what they were shouting, yet he doubted they were singing his praises.

Rafiq had suggested he return at night, yet he'd refused. He might be seriously flawed, but had never been a coward. Whatever he had to endure to fulfill his obligation, he would do so with his head held high and without help.

He thought back to Madison Foster's visit two days ago, as well as her intimation that he might be considered a stranger in a familiar land. He'd come close to accepting her offer, but not for those reasons. She'd simply intrigued him. She'd also forced him to realize how long it had been since he'd kept company with a woman. Yet she would have proven to be too great a temptation, and he could not afford even a hint of a scandal. If they only knew the real scandal that had existed within the palace gates, a secret that had plagued him for seven years, and the primary reason why he'd left.

As the car came to a stop, Zain quickly exited, but he couldn't ignore the shouts of *"Kha'en!"* He could not counter the claims he'd been a traitor without revealing truths he had no intention of disclosing.

Two sentries opened the heavy doors wide, allowing him to evade the crowd's condemnation for the time being. Yet the hallowed halls of the palace were as cold as the stone that comprised them. At one time he'd been happy to call this place home—a refuge steeped in lavish riches and ancient history. Not anymore. But he did welcome the site of the petite woman standing at the end of the lengthy corridor—Elena Battelli, the Italian au pair hired by his father for his sons, despite serious disapproval from the elders. Elena had been his nursemaid, his teacher, his confidante and eventually his surrogate mother following his own mother's untimely death. She'd been the only person who understood his ways, including his wanderlust.

As soon as Zain reached her, Elena opened her arms and smiled. "Welcome back, *caro mio*." She spoke to him in English, as she always had with the Mehdi boys, their "code" when they'd wanted to avoid prying ears.

He drew her into an embrace before stepping back and studying her face. "You are still as elegant as a gazelle, Elena."

She patted her neatly coiffed silver hair. "I am an old gazelle, and you are still the charming *giovinetto* I have always adored." A melancholy look suddenly crossed her face. "Now that your father has sadly left us, and you are to be king, I shall address you as such, Your Majesty."

"Do not even think of it," he said. "You are family and always will be, regardless of my station."

She reached up and patted his cheek. "Yes, that is true. But you are still the king."

"Not officially for another few weeks." That reminded him of his most pressing mission. "Where is Rafiq?"

She shrugged. "In your father's study, *caro*. He has spent most of his time there since…" Her gaze wandered away, but not before Zain glimpsed tears in her eyes.

He leaned and kissed her cheek. "We shall have a long talk soon."

She pulled a tissue from her pocket and dabbed at her eyes. "We shall. You must tell me everything you have been doing while you were away."

He didn't dare tell her everything. He might be an

adult now, but she could still make him feel like the errant schoolboy. "I look forward to our visit."

Ignoring his bodyguards and Deeb, Zain sprinted up the stone steps to his father's second-floor sanctuary and opened the door without bothering to knock. The moment he stepped inside, he thought back to how badly he'd hated this place, plagued by memories of facing his father's ire over crossing lines that he'd been warned not to cross. King Aadil Mehdi had ruled with an iron hand and little heart. And now he was gone.

Zain experienced both guilt and regret that their last words had been spoken in anger. That he hadn't been able to forgive his father for his transgressions. Yet he could not worry about that now. He had more pressing matters that hung over his head like a guillotine.

His gaze came to rest on his brother predictably seated in the king's favorite chair located near the shelves housing several rare collections. The changes in Rafiq were subtle in some ways, obvious in others. He wore the kaffiyeh, which Zain refused to wear, at least for the time being. He also sported a neatly trimmed goatee, much the same as their father's. In fact, Rafiq could be a younger version of the king in every way—both physically and philosophically.

Rafiq glanced up from the newspaper he'd been reading and leveled a nonchalant look on Zain. "I see you have arrived in one piece."

He didn't appreciate his brother's indifference or that he looked entirely too comfortable in the surroundings. "And I see you've taken up residence in the king's official office. Do you plan to stay here indefinitely?"

Rafiq folded the paper in precise creases and tossed it onto the nearby desk. "The question is, brother, do you intend to stay indefinitely, or will this be only a brief visit?"

Zain's anger began to boil below the surface as he attempted to cling to his calm. "Unfortunately for you, as the rightful heir to the throne, I'll be here permanently. I've been preparing for this role for years."

"By bedding women on several continents?"

His composure began to diminish. "Do not pretend to know me, Rafiq."

"I would never presume that, Zain. You have been away for seven years and I only know what I have read about you."

At one time, he and Rafiq had been thick as thieves. Sadly, that had ended when his brother had sided with their father over their differences, leaving brotherly ties in tatters. "I left because our father placed me in an intolerable position."

"He only wanted you to adhere to the rules."

Outdated rules that made no sense in modern times, yet that had only been a small part of his decision. If Rafiq knew the whole story, he might not be so quick to revere their patriarch. "He wanted me to be exactly like him—unwilling to move this country into the millennium because of archaic ideals."

Rafiq rose slowly to his feet and walked to the window to peer outside. "The people are gathered at the gates, along with members of the press. One group demands an explanation as to why their new king deserted them years ago, the other waits for the wayward prince to explain his questionable behavior. Quite the dilemma."

"I will answer those questions in due time." Those that needed answering.

Rafiq turned and frowned. "Are you certain you can handle the pressure?"

If he didn't leave soon, he could possibly throw a punch, producing more fodder for the gossip mill. "Your lack of faith wounds me, brother. Have you ever known a time when I failed to win people over?"

"We are not children any longer, Zain," he said. "You can no longer brandish a smile and a few choice words and expect to prove you are worthy to be king."

He clenched his fists now dangling at his sides. "Yet our father chose me to be king, Rafiq, whether you agree or not."

"Our father believed that designating you as his successor would ensure you would eventually return. And in regard to your current status, you have yet to be officially crowned."

Zain wondered if his brother might be hoping he would abdicate before that time. Never in a million years would he do that. Especially now. "That should be enough time for a seamless transition." If only he felt as confident as he'd sounded.

"There will be serious challenges," Rafiq said. "Our father worked hard to maintain our status as a neutral, autonomous country. Our borders are secure and we have avoided political unrest."

"And we will continue to do so under my reign."

"Only if you can convince your subjects that you have their best interests at heart. Any semblance of unrest will only invite those who would take advantage of the division. That is why I urge you to consider working with Madison Foster."

He should have known it would come back to her. He'd had enough trouble keeping his thoughts away from Madison without the reminder. "Why do you believe her input would be so invaluable?"

"She has been extremely successful in her endeavors," Rafiq said. "She has taken men with political aspirations and serious deficits and restored their honor."

He was growing weary of the insults. "So now my honor is in question?"

"To some degree, yes," Rafiq said as he reclaimed the chair. "What harm would there be in utilizing her talents? Quite frankly, I cannot believe you would refuse the opportunity to spend time with an attractive woman."

As always, most people assumed he had no other concerns than his next conquest. Of course, he couldn't deny that he'd considered the advantages of having Madison involved in his daily routine. Yet that might be dangerous in the long term, unless he wanted to prove everyone right that he could not resist temptation. "Again, I do not wish or need her help."

Rafiq blew out a frustrated sigh. "If you choose the wrong path, Zain, there will be no turning back. If you fail to win over your subjects, you will weaken our country, leaving it open to radical factions bent on taking advantage of our weakness. Is your pride worth possible ruin?"

Zain thought back to the angry voices, the accusations he'd endured moments ago. He hated to concede to his brother's demands, but he did recognize Rafiq's valid concerns. He would find a way to maintain his pride and still accept Madison's assistance—as long as she understood that he would remain completely in charge. Considering the woman's obvious tenacity, that could be a challenge. But then he had always welcomed a good challenge.

If bringing Madison Foster temporarily into the fold kept Rafiq off his back, he saw no harm in giving it a try. "All right. I will give it some thought, but should I decide to accept her assistance, I will only do so if it's understood that I'll dismiss her if she is more hindrance than help."

"Actually, the agreement is already in place, and the terms of her contract state she cannot be dismissed on the grounds of anything other than gross misconduct. That would be my determination, not yours."

Contract? "When did she sign this document?"

"After she contacted me to report on your initial meeting. She is bound to stay until after your coronation, but she insisted on a clause that allows her the option to leave prior to that time should she find the situation intolerable."

His own brother had tied him to a liaison against his will. However, that did not mean he had to be cooperative. "Since you leave me no choice, my first official edict states you will be in charge of the arrangements to bring her here."

Rafiq sent him a victorious smile. "You may consider it done."

As fatigue began to set in, Zain loosened his tie and released the shirt collar's top button. "We'll continue our conversation over dinner." He suddenly remembered he hadn't seen any sign of his youngest brother. "Will Adan be joining us?"

"Adan is currently in the United Kingdom for flight training. He will be returning before the coronation."

Zain couldn't mask his disappointment. "I've been looking forward to seeing him and catching up on his accomplishments. But it's probably best we have no distractions when you bring me up to speed on the council's most recent endeavors."

Rafiq cleared his throat and looked away. "We will not exactly be dining alone."

"Another member of the council?"

"No. A woman."

Zain suspected he might know what this was all about. "Is this someone special in your life?"

"She has no bearing on my life."

He internally cringed. "If this is the beginning of the queen candidate procession, then I—"

"She is not in the market to be your wife."

He did not appreciate his brother's vagueness. "Then who is she, Rafiq?"

"Madison Foster."

Two

"Do you always insist on having your way?"

Startled, Madison shot a glance to her right to discover Zain Mehdi standing in the doorway, one shoulder leaned against the frame, his expression unforgiving on that patently gorgeous face. "Do you always barge in without knocking?" she asked around the surprise attack.

"The door was ajar."

She turned from the bureau, bumped the drawer closed with her butt and tightened the sash on the blue satin robe. "Really? I could have sworn I closed it before I took my shower. But I suppose it could have magically opened on its own, since Arabia is well-known for its magic."

He ignored her sarcasm and walked into the room without an invitation, hands firmly planted in the pockets of his black slacks. With those deadly dark eyes and remarkable physique, the Arabian king could pass for an exotic male model—a model who sorely lacked good comportment.

He strolled to the open armoire to inspect the row of suits, skirts and slacks that Madison had hung only moments before. "As I predicted. Conventional clothing."

His audacity was second only to his arrogance. "It's known as business attire."

"Attire that conceals your true nature," he said as he slid his fingertips down the side of one beige silk skirt.

She couldn't quite explain why she shivered over the gesture, or the sudden, unexpected image of experiencing his touch firsthand. "What do you know about my true nature?"

"I know your kind." He turned and presented a seriously sexy half smile. "Beneath the conservative clothes you wear colorful lingerie."

Lucky guess. "That's a rather huge assumption."

"Am I wrong?"

She refused to confirm or deny his conjecture. "Don't you have some royal duty to perform? Maybe you should have all the locks checked on all the palace doors."

He took a few slow steps toward her. "I'll leave as soon as you tell me why you're here when I made it quite I clear I do not need your help."

She was starting to ask herself the same question. "Your brother's convinced that you need my help."

"Rafiq isn't in charge of my life, nor is he in charge of the country. I am, and I can handle the transition on my own without any assistance."

Oh, but he did need her help, even if he wouldn't admit it. Yet. "From what I witnessed during your arrival, it appears the people aren't welcoming you with open arms."

His expression turned to stone. "As I told you before, Ms. Foster, they have no choice. I am this country's rightful leader and they will have to learn to accept it."

"But wouldn't it be more favorable if you had the blessing of your country's people?"

"And how do you propose to assist me in winning their approval? Do you plan to throw me a parade along with the international cocktail party?"

She mentally added *cynical* to the *sexy* thing. "I suppose we could try that, but a parade isn't successful unless someone shows up. I have several ideas and I hope that you'll at least give me the opportunity to explore those options with you."

"Ah, yes. The social gatherings where you'll be parading me in front of dignitaries."

"We nixed the parade, remember?"

Amusement called out from his dark eyes. "I am still not convinced that you will make an impact on my acceptance."

Time to bring out the legal implications. "As I'm sure your brother told you, the contract states I'll be here until the coronation, whether you choose to work with me or not. Of course, I can't force you to cooperate, but it would be worth your while to at least make the effort."

He seemed to mull that over for a minute while Madison held her breath. "All right. Since you are protected by a legal document, and I've been stripped of my power to dismiss you, I will cooperate on a trial basis. But that cooperation hinges on your ability to meet my terms."

She should have known he'd have an ulterior motive behind his sudden change of heart. "And what would those be?"

His smile returned, slow as a desert sunrise. "I'll let you know in the upcoming days."

Something told Madison his terms could be somewhat suspect. Still, she was more than curious, as well as determined to win him over. "Fine. We can begin tomorrow morning."

"We can begin tonight after dinner," he said, followed by a long visual journey from her neck to her bare feet. "I personally have no objection to your current attire, but something a little less distracting might be more appropriate."

She'd basically forgotten what she was wearing— or wasn't wearing for that matter. "Since I've spent a good deal of time attending state dinners, I know how to dress properly."

He rested one hand on the ornately carved footboard. "This isn't a diplomatic affair, Ms. Foster, only a casual meal."

She felt somewhat uncomfortable having him so close to the bed. "Will both your brothers be dining with us?"

"Only Rafiq. Adan's currently away on a mission."

She was disappointed she wouldn't meet the youngest Mehdi son. "Diplomatic assignment?"

"Military. He's testing a new aircraft."

"That's right. I'd read somewhere he's a pilot."

"Adan's affinity for danger is second only to his appreciation of beautiful women," he said. "He will be greatly disappointed if he does not have the opportunity to meet you."

Maybe it was best if baby brother stayed away for as long as possible. Two womanizers under one roof could be too much to handle. "Will he be back for the coronation?"

Zain pushed away from the bed, allowing Madison to breathe a little easier. "As far as I know."

She hugged her arms closer to her middle. "I'll meet him then."

"If you are still here," he said.

He wasn't going to get rid of her that easily. But she did plan to dismiss him for the time being. "Since it's getting late, I should probably get dressed now."

"Yes, I suppose you should," he said, a hint of fake disappointment in his tone. "I wouldn't mind seeing you in the black dress you have hanging behind your business suits."

He'd been more observant than she realized. "I'll decide what I'm wearing after you're gone."

"You should definitely consider the red lingerie."

Madison didn't understand his fascination with her underwear, or how he'd correctly guessed her fondness for red silk, until she followed his gaze to some focal point at her hip. When she looked down, she saw her bra strap hanging from the closed drawer like a crimson snake in the grass. She quickly stuffed it back inside before pointing toward the door. "Out. Now."

"Dinner is at five-thirty sharp. Do not be late," he said as he walked out the door and closed it behind him.

The man's overbearing behavior equaled his fortune, but he had a thing or two to learn about Madison's determination. She didn't appreciate his observations, even if he had been on target when it came to her clothing. Still, no sexy, bossy sheikh—even if he happened to be a king and her current employer—would dictate her choice in panties. In fact, Zain Mehdi would have nothing whatsoever to do with her panties. And the next time she had him alone, she planned to set him straight about what she expected from him. Namely respect.

The sudden knock indicated she could have an immediate opportunity to do that very thing. On the heels of her frustration, she strode across the room, flung open the door and greeted the offending party with, "More commentary on my underwear?"

When she saw the demure lady with silver hair and topaz eyes standing in the hallway, Madison realized she'd made a colossal mistake. Yet she couldn't seem to speak around her mortification.

"I'm Elena Battelli," the woman said as she extended her hand. "And I am not concerned with your undergarments."

She accepted the gesture and attempted a self-conscious smile. "I'm Madison Foster, and I'm so sorry. I thought you were—"

"Prince Zain, of course."

Realizing her state of undress had only compounded the erroneous assumptions, Madison hugged her arms tightly around her middle. "I know how this must look to you, but His Highness accidentally walked in on me."

The woman sent her a knowing look. "Prince Zain never does anything accidentally."

She wouldn't dispute that point. "Regardless, nothing inappropriate occurred."

"Of course," Elena said, her tone hinting at disbelief. "Do you find your accommodations satisfactory?"

Who wouldn't? The massive marble jetted tub alone was worth any grief Zain Mehdi could hand her. "Very much so, thank you."

She took a slight step back. "Good. Dinner's at six."

"Prince Zain told me five-thirty."

"I am afraid you've been misled," Elena said. "Dinner is always served at 6:00 p.m. That has been the designated time since I've been an employee."

Madison saw the woman as the perfect resource for information on the future king. "How long ago has that been?"

She lifted her chin with pride. "Thirty-four years. I arrived before Prince Zain's birth to assume my role as his *bambinaia,* or in English, his—"

"Nanny," Madison interjected, then added, "I speak Italian. I studied abroad in Florence my sophomore year in college."

Elena's expression brightened. "Excellent. I am from Scandicci."

"I visited there a few times. It's a beautiful place. Do you go back often?"

All the joy seemed to drain from Elena's face. "Not as often as I would like. My life is here with the royal family."

A royal family with adult sons who no longer needed a nanny. A keeper, maybe, but not a nursemaid. "How do you spend your days now that the princes are grown?"

"I am basically in charge of running the household while waiting for my opportunity to raise another generation of Mehdi children."

Madison didn't quite see Zain as father material, an opinion she'd keep to herself. "I'm sure you gained invaluable experience with Prince Zain."

"Yes, yet clearly I failed to impress upon him the merits of self-control when it comes to the opposite sex. Otherwise, he would not be interested in your undergarments."

They shared in a brief laugh before Madison revealed her opinion on the subject. "I assure you, Prince Zain will not be commenting on my personal effects if I have any say in the matter."

Elena presented a sly smile. "A word of advice. Prince Zain is a good man, yet he is still a man. What he lacks in restraint, he makes up in charm. Stand firm with him."

With that, she walked away, leaving Madison to ponder exactly what the future king might have up his sleeve when he'd told her the incorrect time for dinner. She highly doubted he'd forgotten standard palace protocol in spite of his lengthy absence. Perhaps he was simply trying to throw her off balance in order to be rid of her.

Too bad. She would definitely stand her ground with him from this point forward. And as far as dinner went, she'd ignore his edict and show up when she darn well pleased.

She was fifteen minutes late, yet Zain wasn't at all surprised. Madison Foster possessed an extreme need to be in control. Granted, he had the means to break down her defenses, and he was tempted to try. Nothing overt. Nothing more than a subtle and slight seduction designed to make her uncomfortable enough to bow out and return to the States where she belonged.

However, she could very well turn the tables by responding to his advances. Possible, but not likely, he decided when she entered the dining room wearing a slim black skirt that came right above her knees, conservative heels and a simple white blouse. A blouse sheer enough to reveal the outline of an equally white bra, most likely in an effort to prove her point. But he knew better. That professional, prim and proper persona only served to conceal the daring beneath her cool exterior. He'd wager the kingdom she had on a pair of brightly colored panties. Red panties.

A richly detailed fantasy assaulted him, one that involved sitting beside her and running his hand up the inside of her thigh and—

"Where would you like me?"

He thought of several answers, none of them appropriate. He chose the least suggestive one. "Are you referring to the seating arrangements, or do you have something else in mind?"

She approached the table and sent him a false smile. "Let me rephrase for the sake of clarity. Where do you want me to be seated?"

Zain gestured to the right of where he was positioned at the head of the lengthy table. "Here." He waited for her to slide into the chair before he launched into his reprimand. "You're late."

She made an exaggerated show of checking her watch. "Actually, I'm fifteen minutes early, since it seems, according to Elena, dinner is and always has been at six."

He'd been betrayed by his former governess and longtime confidante. "Now that I will soon assume my rightful role as king, dinner will be at five-thirty."

She folded her hands atop the table, her gaze unwavering. "I suppose having your first royal edict involving dinnertime is preferable to, oh, say, changing the entire governmental structure."

"That will be my second royal edict."

She looked sincerely confused. "Are you serious?"

He smiled. "Not entirely, but I do plan to implement some much-needed change."

"Change cannot occur until you are officially crowned, brother."

Zain pulled his gaze from Madison to see Rafiq claiming his place at the opposite end of the table. "As disappointing as it might be to you, *brother,* that will happen in a matter of weeks. In the meantime, I plan to outline those changes to the council later this week."

Rafiq lifted his napkin and placed it in his lap. "I have no designs on your position, Zain. But I do have a vested interest in the direction in which you plan to take my country."

He fisted his hands on the heels of his anger. "*Our* country, Rafiq. A country that I plan to lead into the twenty-first century."

Madison cleared her throat, garnering their attention. "What's for dinner?"

"Cheeseburgers in your honor."

When he winked, she surprisingly smiled. "I was truly looking forward to sampling some Middle Eastern fare," she said.

"We're having the chef's special kebabs," Rafiq said. "You will have to excuse my brother's somewhat questionable sense of humor, Ms. Foster."

After shooting Rafiq an acid look, Zain regarded Madison again. "I believe you'll agree that a questionable sense of humor is better than no sense of humor at all."

She shifted slightly in her seat. "I enjoyed meeting Elena. Will she be joining us?"

"Not tonight," Rafiq said as one of the staff circled the table and poured water. "She has some work to attend to, but she sends her apologies."

"She works much too hard," Zain added. "I plan to put an end to that and soon."

Rafiq leaned back in his chair. "I am afraid her work will not let up until after the coronation and the wedding."

"Wedding?" Madison asked, the shock in her tone matching Zain's.

"And who is the lucky bride?" Zain asked, though he suspected he knew the answer.

"Rima Acar, of course," Rafiq said. "We will be married the week before the coronation."

Zain wasn't at all surprised by the news his brother was going through with the long-standing marriage contract. He was surprised—and angry—over the timing.

"Is this wedding a means to detract from my assuming my rightful place as king?"

"Of course not," Rafiq said. "This wedding has been in the planning stages for years. Almost twelve if you consider when Father and the sultan came to an agreement."

"Ah, yes, the age-old tradition of bride bartering." Zain turned his attention back to Madison, who seemed intent on pushing fruit around on her plate. "We are destined to choose a wife from the highest bidder. Someone who will give us many heirs, if not passion."

"As you, too, had your bride chosen for you," Rafiq added.

Madison's blue eyes went wide. "You're engaged?"

"Not any longer," Rafiq said. "Zain's intended grew tired of waiting for his return and married another."

He had thanked his good fortune for that many times over. "Her decision was for the best. I refuse to wed a woman whom I've never met, let alone kissed." He leaned forward and leveled his gaze on his brother. "Have you kissed Rima? Have you determined there will be enough passion to sustain your marriage? Or do you even care?"

He could see the fury brewing in Rafiq's eyes. "That is none of your concern. Passion is not important. Continuing the royal lineage is."

"Procreating would be rather difficult if you cannot bear to touch your wife, brother. Or perhaps you will be satisfied with bedding her only enough times to make a child, as it was with our own parents."

"Do not believe everything you hear, Zain. Our parents had a satisfactory marriage."

Rafiq—always their father's defender. "Satisfactory?

Are you also going to dispute that the king played a part in our mother's—"

Rafiq slammed his palm on the table, rattling the dinnerware. "That is enough."

Zain tossed his napkin aside and ignored the woman setting the entrée before him. "I agree. I have had enough of this conversation." He came to his feet and regarded Madison. "Ms. Foster, my apologies for disrupting your meal."

Without even a passing glance at his brother, Zain left the room and took the stairs two at a time. He had no doubt that after the display of distasteful family dynamics, he would have no need to seduce Madison Foster. She would most likely be taking the first plane back to America.

With a plate balanced in her left hand, Madison knocked with her right and waited to gain entry, affording the king the courtesy he hadn't shown her earlier that afternoon.

"Enter" sounded from behind the heavy wooden door, the gruff, masculine voice full of obvious frustration.

Madison strode into the room, head held high, determined not to show even a speck of nervousness, though admittedly she was a little shaky. More than a little shaky when she met his stern gaze and realized he didn't look at all thrilled to see her.

She set the plate on the desk and sat across from him without waiting for an invitation. "Elena sent you some pasta and the message that if you don't eat, you'll be too weak to rule."

He didn't bother to stand. Instead, he stared at her for a few moments before he pushed the offering away. "You may tell Elena I will eat when I'm hungry."

She'd been stuck in the middle of one argument too many today. "You can tell her. Right now, we need to discuss your upcoming plans."

He leaned back in the brown leather chair and tented his hands together. "I assumed you would be well on your way home by now."

"You assumed wrong. I'm determined to see this through."

"Even after we aired our family grievances at dinner?"

He had a lot to learn about her tenacity. "I've heard worse, and now I'd like to ask you a few questions."

"Proceed."

She would, with caution. "Do you have a strategy for overcoming your playboy reputation?"

"My reputation has been overblown, Ms. Foster."

"Perception is everything when it comes to politics, Your Highness. And believe what you will, you're in a political battle to restore your people's faith in you. You've been gone almost ten years—"

"Seven years."

"If you were a dog, that's equivalent to almost fifty years." And that had to be the most inane thing she'd said in ages, if ever. "Not that you're a dog. I'm only saying that seven years is a long time in your situation."

He hinted at a smile. "Do you own a dog?"

"Yes, I do. I mean, I did." Clearly he was trying to divert her attention from more pressing concerns by using her former pooch. "Could we please get back on point?"

"Yes," he said. "The point is I am quite capable of overcoming my exaggerated reputation by demonstrating there is more to my character."

He was so sure of himself. So sexy in his confidence, and she hated herself for noticing. Again. "Can you really do that? Can you persuade the world you're a serious leader when you can't even convince your own brother you're committed to your duty?"

His dark eyes relayed an intense anger. "What did Rafiq tell you when I left the table?"

Not as much as she would've liked. "He only said that he's worried you'll take off again if the pressure becomes too great."

"Despite what my brother believes, I am not a coward."

"I don't think anyone is calling you a coward." She sighed. "Look, I realize you have a lot of pride, but you might want to give up a little and realize you need someone in your corner. Someone who can serve as a sounding board during this transition."

"And you are that someone?"

"I can be. And if you'll allow me to use my connections, I can help establish some allies, and every country needs those. Even small, autonomous countries. I also still contend that you could use some help with your public addresses." When he started to speak, she held up her hand to silence him. "I know, you have a degree and you're intelligent and articulate, but I don't see the harm in brainstorming content."

"I still see no reason why I would need to consult anyone on what I wish to say or how I wish to say it."

She was making no headway whatsoever. "What about the press? Wouldn't you like to have someone serve as a buffer to make certain they convey the proper message?"

"I have Deeb for that."

Deeb had about as much personality as a paperweight. "But if you show the world that you have a woman at your side, and one you're not engaging in a torrid affair, that would send a clear message you're not the player everyone believes you to be."

He studied the ceiling and remained silent for a few seconds before he brought his attention back to her. "Should we proceed, I have to be assured that whatever you might hear or might learn within these sacred walls will not be repeated."

Madison sensed impending victory, and possibly some serious secrets. "You can trust me to maintain confidentiality at all costs. But I have to know if there's a scandal that could surface in the foreseeable future."

"Not if I can prevent it. And at the moment, that is all you need to know."

Madison could only hope that he might eventually trust her enough to confide in her. Otherwise, she couldn't prepare for the worst-case scenario. "Fine. Then you agree to accept my help?"

He streaked a palm over his shaded jaw. "For the time being, and as I stated earlier, you must agree to my terms."

Clearly he needed to maintain control. She'd give him a little leeway for now. "Fine. Perhaps now would be a good time to spell out your terms."

"If I disagree with your advice, you'll refrain from arguing," he said.

That could prove to be a challenge. "Okay."

"You will consult me before you plan your soirées, and you will let me approve the guest lists."

Considering his lack of popularity, it could prove to be a short list. "Fair enough."

"And you will adhere to my schedule, which means I will decide the time and the place for our meetings."

"I assumed your study would be the most appropriate meeting place."

"It might be necessary to find a more private venue."

Now she had her own terms to present. "As long as it's not your bedroom."

He smiled. "You're not the least bit curious about my royal quarters?"

Oh, yes, she was. "No. Anything else?"

He feigned disappointment. "I'll let you know as soon as I've determined what I expect beyond what we've already discussed."

Talk about being vague. But she'd accept vague as long as she could continue as planned. "We'll go over your upcoming schedule in the morning, Your Highness, and plan accordingly."

"Call me Zain."

Her mouth momentarily dropped open over the request. "That's a bit too informal, don't you think?"

"When we're alone, I want you to call me by my given name. Otherwise, our agreement terminates immediately."

What kind of game was he playing? Only time would tell, and Madison hoped she didn't find herself on the losing end.

She came to her feet and tugged at the hem of her blouse. "Whatever floats your boat, *Zain*. Now if you'll excuse me, I'm going to my room to relax."

"You are excused. For now."

Madison had only made it a few steps toward the door before Zain uttered the single word. "Black."

She turned and frowned. "Excuse me?"

"You're wearing black lingerie."

Did the man have X-ray vision? "Why are you so fascinated with my underwear?"

His grin arrived slowly. "Am I correct?"

She folded her arms beneath her breasts. "That's for me to know—"

"And for me to find out?"

She should've known he'd been in America long enough to learn all the little sayings. "That's for me to know, period. Anything else? Or would you like to discuss *your* royal underwear?"

His grin deepened. "I have nothing to hide."

That remained to be seen. She intended to leave well enough alone before she was tempted to abandon the good-sense ship. Before she gave in to the tiny little spark of awareness or the slight full-body shiver brought about by his deadly smile. "I'm going now."

He finally rose from the chair. "I suggest you watch the sunset from the terrace outside your room. I'll have Elena send up some of her special tea to help you relax."

She'd be more relaxed as soon as she got away from all his charisma. "What kind of tea?"

"I'm not certain," he said as he strolled toward her and stopped only a foot or so away. "I've never tried it. I do know it is formulated to help a person sleep."

She'd probably have no trouble sleeping the moment her head hit the pillow. "Thank you, and I'll see you in the morning."

"You're welcome." He reached out and pushed a strand of hair behind her ear. "If the tea doesn't help you sleep, my room is next door to yours. Feel free to wake me."

"What for?" As if she really had to ask.

"Whatever you need to help you relax."

She suddenly engaged in one heck of a naked-body fantasy that made her want to run for cover. "I assure you I won't need anything to help me relax."

"Let me know if you change your mind."

"I won't be changing my mind." She turned toward the door then faced him again when something dawned on her. "By the way, if all this innuendo is some ploy to scare me off, save your breath. I've been propositioned by the best." And the worst of the worst.

He looked almost crestfallen. "I'm wounded you would think I would resort to such underhanded tactics."

Maybe she had overreacted a tad. Some men just happened to be blessed with the flirtation gene. "My apologies if I'm wrong about your motives."

"Actually, you are correct," he said. "That was my original plan. But you have bested me, so I promise to behave myself from this point forward."

She had a hard time believing that. "Well, in case you should get any more bright ideas, just know it will take more than a few well-rehearsed, suggestive lines to send me packing. I've spent many years studying human nature, and I know what you're all about."

He braced a hand on the doorframe above her head. "Enlighten me, Madison."

The sound of her name rolling softly out of his mouth, his close proximity, was not helping her concentration. "You use your charm to discourage perceived threats to your control, and to encourage the results you wish to achieve, namely driving people away. But beneath all that sexy macho bravado, I believe you're a man with a great deal of conviction when it comes to his country's future. Am I correct?"

"Perhaps you are only projecting your need for control on me. I believe at times giving up control to another is preferable. Have you never been tempted to throw out logic and act on pure instinct?"

Her instincts told her he wasn't referring to a professional relationship. "Not when it comes to mixing business with pleasure, if that's what you're asking. Don't forget we're trying to repair your reputation, not enhance it."

He had the nerve to show his pearly whites to supreme advantage. "Sometimes the pleasure is worth the risk."

"I thought you promised to behave."

He straightened and attempted to look contrite. "My apologies. I was momentarily struck senseless by your analysis."

Before she was momentarily struck stupid and kissed that smug, sexy smile off his face, Madison made a hasty exit.

She hadn't lied when she'd admitted she'd been propositioned before. She *had* lied when she'd claimed she hadn't been tempted to cross professional lines, because she had—the moment she'd reunited with Zain Mehdi.

Three

Perception is everything...

Zain had to agree with Madison on that point. He'd always been perceived as a man with a strong affinity for attractive women, a fact he could not deny. Yet that standing had provided the means to carry out his covert activities over the past seven years, and earned him the Phantom Sheikh title. His absence had always been blamed on a lover, and most of the time that had been far from the truth. *Most* of the time. He hadn't been celibate by any means, but he had not had as many affairs as what the media had led people to believe. If he had, he would have been perpetually sleep deprived.

He also recognized that giving in to temptation with a woman like Madison Foster—an intelligent, beautiful and somewhat willful woman—could possibly lead to disaster. Still, he wasn't one to easily ignore temptation, even if wisdom dictated that he must. And at the moment, Madison looked extremely tempting.

Zain remained in the open doorway to his suite in order to study her. She stood at the veranda's stone wall, looking out over the valley below, her golden hair flowing down her back. She'd exchanged her conservative clothing for more comfortable attire—a casual gauze skirt and a loose magenta top that revealed one slim, bare shoulder. He didn't need to venture a guess as to the color of her bra, since she didn't appear to be wearing one. That thought alone had him reconsidering the merits of wisdom.

Zain cleared his throat as he approached her, yet she didn't seem to notice his presence. Not until he said, "It's a remarkable view, isn't it?"

She sent him a backward glance and a slight scowl. "Why do you keep sneaking up on me?"

He moved beside her, leaving a comfortable distance between them. "My apologies. I did not intend to startle you. I only wanted to make certain you have everything you need from me."

She faced him, leaned a hip against the wall and rolled her eyes. "Are we back to that again?"

"My intentions are completely innocent." Only a half-truth. He'd gladly give her anything she needed in a carnal sense.

She took a sip from the cup clutched in her hands. "Sorry, but I'm having trouble buying the innocent act after your recent admission."

That came as no surprise to Zain, and he probably deserved her suspicions. "I will do my best to earn your trust." He nodded toward the cup. "I gather that's Elena's special tea."

"Yes, it is, and it's very good."

"Do you have any idea what might be in it?"

She lifted that bare shoulder in a shrug and took a sip. "I suspect it's chamomile and some other kind of herb. I can taste mint."

He turned toward her and rested one elbow on the stone barrier. "Take care with how much you drink. It could be more than tea."

"Too late. This is my third cup, and do you mean alcohol?"

"Precisely."

"Is that allowed?" she asked.

"Elena is free to do as she pleases, as is everyone else in the country, within reason. We've always had a spiritually, economically and culturally diverse population, due in part to people entering the borders seeking—"

"Asylum?"

"And peace."

She turned back to the view and surveyed the scene. "Then Bajul is the Switzerland of the Middle East?"

"In a manner of speaking. I might not have agreed with all my father's philosophies, but I've always admired his determination to remain neutral in a volatile region. Unfortunately, the threat to end our peaceful co-existence still exists, as it always has. As it is everywhere else in the world."

She took another drink and set the cup aside. "The landscape is incredible. I hadn't expected Bajul to be so green or elevated."

"You expected desert."

"Honestly, yes, I did."

Another example of inaccurate perception. "If you go north, you'll find the desert. Go south and you'll find the sea."

She sighed. "I love the sea. I love water, period."

He took the opportunity to move a little closer, his arm pressed against hers as he pointed toward the horizon. "Do you see that mountain rising between two smaller peaks?"

She shaded her eyes against the setting sun. "The skinny one that looks almost phallic?"

That made him smile. "It is known as Mabrúruk, our capital city's namesake. Legend has it that Al-'Uzzá, a mythological goddess, placed it there to enhance fertility. Reportedly her efforts have been successful, from crops to livestock to humans."

"Interesting," she said. "Do people have to go to the mountain to procreate, or does it have a long radius?" She followed the comment with a soft, sensual laugh. "No pun intended."

Discussing procreation with her so close only made Zain's fantasies spring to life, among other things. "I suppose it's possible, but that's not the point I was trying to make."

She turned and leaned a hip against the wall. "What point were you trying to make, Your Highness?"

She seemed determined to disregard his terms. "Zain."

Madison blew out a long breath. "What were you going to say before the topic turned to the baby-making mountain, *Zain?*"

He liked the breathless way she said his name. He liked the way she looked at the moment—slightly disheveled and extremely sensual. "I was going to point out that beyond the ridge there are two lakes. Perhaps I'll take you there in the near future."

"That would be nice, as long as you don't expect any baby making."

He certainly wouldn't mind making love to her in the

shadow of the mountain, or perhaps in the lake. Without the resulting baby, of course.

He forced his thoughts back to business matters. "My intent would be to show you the key to Bajul's future."

"What would that be?"

"Water."

She appeared to be confused. "For a fishery?"

"Food and water are commodities in the region," he explained. "We have more rain than most, and our lakes have deep aquifers. They also have the capacity to sustain our land for many years to come, and that means bountiful crops and livestock. Those commodities could serve as an export for countries that suffer shortages as long as we make certain we protect our resources. My plans include exploring innovative and eco-friendly ways to treat and preserve the water from the lakes."

She laid her palm on his arm. "That sounds like a wonderful plan, Zain."

The simple touch sent a surge of heat coursing through his body. "That plan will not come to fruition unless I can convince the council it's our best recourse as opposed to oil."

She unfortunately took her hand away. "But you'll have your brother's support, correct?"

If only that were true. "He'll be the hardest to convince. He will most likely side with the council and suggest drilling as soon as possible. I refuse to allow that unless we have exhausted all alternatives."

"I don't understand why the two of you seem to butt horns at every turn."

This would require more than a brief explanation, yet he felt she had the right to know. "Most believe that the crown automatically passes to the firstborn son. In my family's case, the reigning king can designate a successor, and he designated me, not Rafiq. My brother has resented that decision for years."

She shook her head. "I guess I assumed Rafiq was younger, although he does seem older in many ways. Not in appearance, because the resemblance between the two of you is remarkable. But he's very stoic."

"He's thirteen months older," he said. "And he is serious about preserving traditions that should be deemed obsolete in this day and time."

"I take it you're referring to arranged marriages."

Unfortunately, that was one change he wasn't prepared to make, even if it impacted his own future. "The tradition of selecting a bride with a royal heritage is necessary. Only a member of royalty can understand the royal life."

"Of course, and keeping the blood blue must be very important."

He ignored the bitterness in her tone. "I know how antiquated it might sound, but yes, that does hold some importance."

"Then why did you give your brother such a hard time about it?"

"Because I do not believe in committing to someone if you haven't explored an intimate relationship prior to committing to marriage. I would never have bought my Bugatti without test-driving it first."

Her eyes went wide. "You're comparing a woman to a car?"

"No. I am only saying that sexual compatibility holds great importance in a marriage, or it should. How will you know you are compatible in that regard unless you experience intimacy before you make a commitment?"

She looked skeptical and borderline angry. "In my

opinion, sex shouldn't carry too much weight. As they say, passion does have a tendency to fade."

"You sound as if you speak from experience. Have you been married?"

"No, but I was in a long-term relationship, and he's the reason I no longer have my dog."

"So you parted because of a canine?"

She briefly smiled. "We were the cliché. He wanted a house and kids and to live in suburbia, while I wanted a career in the city."

"And you have no desire to have a family?"

An odd and fleeting look of pain crossed her expression. "I have no intention of giving up my career for a man. My mother fell into that trap with my father."

Her past obviously was as complex as his. "That wasn't the life she chose?"

She downed the rest of the tea. "Oh, she chose it, all right. She gave up a career as a medical researcher to globe-trot with her diplomat husband. I've never understood how someone could claim to love someone so much that they'd set their aspirations aside for another person."

"Perhaps it all goes back to shared and sustained passion."

She released a sarcastic laugh. "Sorry, but I just can't wrap my mind around that. In fact, I don't even want to think about passion and my parents in the same sentence."

Her skepticism both surprised and intrigued him. "Have you never experienced a strong passion for someone?"

"As I've said, it's overrated."

Apparently she hadn't been with the right man. A man who could show her the true meaning of desire.

He could be that man. He wanted to be that man despite his original intention to drive her away. And so went the last of his wisdom.

He surveyed her face from forehead to chin and centered on her mouth. "You've never been so attuned to someone that when you enter a room, that person is all you see? You've never wanted someone so desperately that you would risk everything to have them?"

She drew in a shaky breath. "Not that I recall."

"I cannot imagine you would have voluntarily missed out on all that lovemaking has to offer."

Her eyes took on a hazy cast. "What makes you think I have missed out?"

He traced her lips with a fingertip. "If you had, you wouldn't be so quick to dismiss the existence of phenomenal sex."

He expected her to argue the point. He predicted she would back away. He wasn't prepared when she gripped the back of his neck and brought his mouth to hers.

All her untapped passion came out in the kiss. He could taste the mint on her tongue, could sense any latent resistance melt when he tightened his hold on her. He had no doubt she could feel how much he wanted her when he streamed his hands to her hips and nudged her completely against him.

He should halt the insanity before he carried her to his bed, or dispensed with formality and took her down where they now stood. Yet stopping didn't appear to be an option—until she stopped.

Madison wrested out of his arms, looking stunned and well kissed and quite perturbed. "What was that?"

Zain leaned back against the wall and dared to smile. "That was uncontrolled passion. I suppose I shouldn't be surprised you didn't recognize it."

She backed up a few steps and tugged at the hem of her blouse. "I tell you what that was. That was a huge mistake on my part. That was too much talk about that darn baby-making mountain."

When she spun around and listed to one side, he clasped her arm to prevent her from falling. "Perhaps it was the tea," he whispered in her ear from behind her.

"Perhaps I'm just an idiot." She pulled away again and spun around to face him. "I'm going to bed now."

"Do you wish some company?" he asked as she backed toward her room.

"Yes... No, I don't wish any company."

With that, she turned and disappeared through the glass door, leaving Zain alone with a strong urge to follow her, and an erection that would take hours to calm.

Now that he'd sampled what Madison Foster had to offer aside from her political expertise, he didn't want her to leave yet. He wanted more. He wanted it all.

She wanted to scream. She wanted to pull the covers over her head and forget what had happened the evening before. She wanted to tell the person who was knocking to go away and come back in day or so. Maybe by then she would be over her mortification enough to make an appearance.

Instead, Madison shoved the heavy eggplant-colored spread aside, left the bed and put on her robe on the way to answer the summons. If she happened to encounter the reason behind her current distress, she just might have to give him another piece of what was left of her mind. Or invite him in...

She yanked open the door to discover Elena once again standing on the threshold, tray in hand and a cheerful smile on her face. "Good morning, Miss Foster. Did you sleep well?"

"Like a rock." Like the dead or better still, the drunk. "What was in that tea, Elena?"

She breezed into the room and set the tray on a table near the glass doors. "Chamomile and a few other things."

Madison tightened her robe. "What other things?"

Elena straightened and swept a hand through her silver hair. "Some herbs and honey and schnapps."

Schnapps. That explained a lot. "You should have warned me. I drank three cups and had to take a twenty-minute shower to sober up before I could find the bed."

"My apologies, *cara*. I only wanted to aid you in relaxing."

"I was definitely relaxed." So much so she'd melted right into Zain's mouth.

Elena pointed in the direction of Madison's chin. "I have a special balm that will help with that irritation."

Confused, Madison strode to the mirrored dresser to take a look. Not only was her hair a blond Medusa mess from going to bed with it wet, she had a nice red patch of whisker burn below her bottom lip. "I used something new on my face, so that must be it. I'll be avoiding it from now on." Avoiding Zain's seduction skills, even if she couldn't avoid him.

"Would this something new be tall, dark and have a heavy evening beard?"

She met Elena's wily smile in the reflection. She hated to lie, so she'd simply be evasive. Turning from the mirror, she gestured toward the tray holding a silver pot and a plate of pastries. "I hope that's not more tea."

Elena shook her head. "No. It's coffee. Very strong

coffee. I decided you would need some caffeine for your meeting with Prince Zain."

She didn't recall scheduling a specific time. Then again, last night's details were a bit fuzzy, except for the blasted kiss. "When does he expect me?"

"Now. He's is in the study, waiting. And he seems to be in a somewhat foul mood."

Lovely. "Do you know the reason behind his foul mood?"

Elena tapped her chin with a slender finger and looked thoughtful. "Perhaps it is because he has tried something new on his face and he would like more of the same."

Madison internally cringed. If she kept backing herself into corners, she'd soon be folded in half. "Elena, seriously, this is just a rash. I have very sensitive skin."

"Yes, *cara,* and I am the Queen of Italia. I can tell when a woman has been kissed, and kissed well. And of course, I know Prince Zain is the culprit. He is a charmer, that *diavoletto.*"

Little devil was an apt description of Zain Mehdi. *Sexy little devil.* "Okay, if you must know, we shared a friendly kiss. Thanks to your special tea, I had a temporary lapse in judgment."

Elena laughed softly. "Prince Zain's powers of persuasion are much stronger than my tea. I only caution you to take care with your heart."

Madison held up her hand as if taking an oath. "I promise you there will be no more kissing, friendly or otherwise. I'm not one to bend the rules, much less break them."

Elena smiled. "I wish you much luck with that." She headed for the door and paused with her hand on the knob. *"L'amore domina senza regole,"* she muttered before she disappeared into the corridor.

Love rules without rules.

Who said anything about love? She wasn't in love with Zain Mehdi. In lust maybe, but that fell far from love.

Regardless, she didn't have time to ponder the woman's warning or the kiss or anything else for that matter. She needed to prepare to see the future king.

After she completed her morning ritual, Madison applied some makeup and twisted and secured her crazy hair at her nape. She dressed in brown slacks and sleeveless beige silk turtleneck that she covered with a taupe jacket, intentionally making certain she bared no skin aside from her hands and face. Wearing gloves and a veil would probably be overkill. She chose to nix the pastry but paused long enough to drink a cup of black lukewarm coffee. Even if she was somewhat hungry, she didn't dare feed the butterflies flitting around in her belly.

Those butterflies continued to annoy her as she grabbed her briefcase and headed downstairs to the second-floor office. Surprisingly she found the door partially ajar, but no guards and no prince in sight when she entered the vacant study. Only a few seconds passed before Zain emerged from what appeared to be an en suite bathroom.

Aside from one wayward lock of dark hair falling across his forehead, he looked every bit the debonair businessman. He wore a pair of black wool slacks and a white shirt with a gray tie draped loosely around his neck. The light shading of whiskers surrounding his mouth led Madison right down the memory path toward that toe-curling kiss.

She shoved the thoughts away and put on a sunny smile. "Good morning."

Without returning the greeting, Zain crossed the room

to the coat tree to the right of the desk and took a jacket from one hanger. "Did you have breakfast?" he asked.

He was so absolutely gorgeous she'd love to have him for breakfast. And lunch. And dinner… "I didn't have time. But I did have the most important staple—coffee."

He turned, slipped the coat on and nailed her with those lethal dark eyes. "I'll have the chef prepare you something you can eat while you wait."

"Wait for what?"

"I am about to address my royal subjects."

Several key concerns tumbled around in Madison's mind. She'd begin with the first. "Best I recall, you're not scheduled to do that for another two days."

He slid the top button closed on his collar. "Apparently the masses did not receive the memo."

Apparently. "Where is this going to take place?"

He gestured to his right. "Outside on the terrace where my father and my father's father have always spoken to the people."

Madison set her briefcase on a chair and immediately walked to the double doors to peek through the heavy red curtains. She saw a substantial stone balcony containing a podium with a skinny microphone as well as several stern—and heavily armed—sentries standing guard. As she peered in the distance, she caught a glimpse of an iron fence, also lined with guards, holding back the milling crowd. And in that crowd stood a few respectable correspondents, along with more than a few pond-scum tabloid reporters.

After dropping the curtain, she faced Zain again. "Do you know what you're going to say?"

He rounded the desk, leaned back against it and began to work his tie. "I am your new king. Accept it."

Her mouth dropped open momentarily from shock. "You can't be serious."

"It is simple and to the point." His smile was crooked, and so was his tie.

"Perhaps a little too simple and too pointed."

"I am not yet prepared to speak on all my plans."

"But are you prepared for the questions that are going to be hurled at you by reporters?"

He buttoned his coat closed. "Rest assured I've handled the press before."

"Even paparazzi?"

"Especially paparazzi."

Considering his notorious way with women, she supposed he probably had encountered more than his share of media stalkers. However, she still worried he could get bombarded by a few queries that could trip him up. Hopefully he'd learned how to ignore those. Too bad his tie was too askew for her to ignore.

Without giving it a second thought, Madison walked right up to him to fix the problem. The memory of her mother doing the same thing for Madison's dad settled over her. Was she in danger of becoming her mother? Only if she professed her undying love to Zain and promised to follow him throughout the world. He wasn't the undying-love kind, but he certainly did smell great. Nothing overpowering, just a hint of light, earthy cologne. Or maybe it was the soap he'd used in the shower. Never before had she aspired to be a bar of soap, but at the moment she did. How nice it would be to travel down all that slick, wet, fantastic male terrain, over muscle and sinew and hills and valleys. Definitely hills…

"Are you finished yet?"

Zain's question jarred Madison back into the here and now. "Almost." She smoothed her hand over the gray silk tie and straightened lapels that didn't need straightening. Just when she was about to step back, he captured her hands against his chest.

"I am curious about something," he said, his dark eyes leveled on hers.

"Sage-green satin. Matching bra, if you must know." Heavens, she was volunteering underwear info before he'd officially asked.

"Actually, I was about to inquire about your night and if you slept well."

Now she felt somewhat foolish and confused as to why she hadn't tried to wrest her hands away from his. "I slept well, thank you, although I did have a few odd dreams."

He raised a brow. "Sexual dreams?"

"Strange dreams. I was climbing up a mountain chasing a snake."

His smile caught her off guard. "Some believe climbing denotes a craving for intercourse. Need I say what the mountain and snake symbolize?"

That phallic mountain would be her Waterloo if they didn't stop discussing it. "Spoken like a man. I'm sure you could make a dream about doing laundry all about sex."

"Perhaps if it involved washing your lingerie."

She tried to hold back her own smile, without success. "Right now you should be concentrating on your speech, not sex dreams."

He raised her hand and kissed her palm before setting it back against his chest. "It's difficult to concentrate with this ongoing chemistry between us."

She couldn't argue that, although she would. "Don't be ridiculous."

"Don't be naive, Madison. You feel it now."

She admittedly did feel a bit warm and somewhat tingly. Maybe a little lightheaded, but then that could be some lingering effects of the tea. She managed to slip from his grasp and take a much-needed step back. "If you're referring to what happened last night, that was a mistake."

"You're going to deny that you wanted to kiss me? That you want to kiss me now?"

She could deny—and lie—in the same breath. "I want to get back to the issue at hand, namely your speech. In my opinion, it's important that you appear to be a strong yet compassionate leader. Be decisive but not forceful."

"I have come to one important decision now."

She folded her arms beneath her breasts. "What would that be?"

He moved closer, rested a hand on her shoulder and brought his lips to her ear. He whispered soft words that sounded lyrical, sensual, though she couldn't begin to comprehend the message, at least not literally. She could venture a guess that the missive was sexual in nature.

When Zain pulled back and homed in on her gaze, she released a slow, ragged breath. "Do you care to interpret what you just said to me?"

"Later, when we have complete privacy."

That sent Madison's imagination straight into overdrive and would have quite possibly, had it not been for the rap on the door, sent Madison straight into Zain's arms.

"Enter," he said, his voice somewhat raspy and noticeably strained.

Madison smoothed a hand down her jacket then over her hair as Deeb stepped in the room, looking every bit the humorless assistant. "You are cleared to proceed, Emir."

Zain rubbed a hand over his jaw. "The shooters are in place?"

"Yes. Four positioned on the roof, two in the tower."

The reality of Zain's importance suddenly hit home for Madison. So did the reality of what she'd almost done—kiss the king for the second time in less than twenty-four hours. Yet she didn't have time to think about it as two bodyguards swept into the room, pulled back the curtains and escorted Zain onto the terrace.

Madison stood to one side slightly behind the drapes while Mr. Deeb took his place beside her. When Zain positioned himself behind the podium, a series of shouts ensued above the murmuring crowd. "What are they saying?" she asked Deeb.

"They are calling him a turncoat."

Ouch. She wished she could see Zain's face, gauge his reaction, but she could only see his back and his hands gripping the edge of the wooden surface, indicating he could be stressed. But no one would know that, she realized, the moment he began to speak in words she couldn't begin to understand.

"What's he saying?" she asked Deeb who remained his usual noncommittal self.

"He is telling them he is honored to be their leader and he looks forward to serving them."

So far, so good. But then she heard the sounds of disapproval and didn't feel nearly as confident. "What now?"

"He claims he is not his father and that he will rule differently," Deeb said. "He is also speaking of positive changes he wishes to make, such as improvements to the hospital and the schools."

As Zain continued, Madison noticed the temporarily dissatisfied crowd had quieted and many people, particularly women, seemed to hang on his every word. And although she couldn't interpret his words, she could certainly appreciate his voice—a deep, mellow voice that went down as smoothly as a vintage glass of wine.

After an enthusiastic round of applause, she turned to ask for clarification from Deeb, only to hear someone suddenly shout in English, "Is it true you fathered a child with Keeley Winterlind?"

Though she'd been aware of Zain's liaison with the supermodel, Madison was seriously stunned by the query, and thoroughly appalled that someone would interrupt a king's speech in search of a sordid story. Worse, was it true?

Zain ignored the question and continued to speak to the throng that seemed to grow more restless by the minute. Then another reporter demanded he address the pregnancy issue, prompting shouts from the masses.

Although Madison still couldn't see Zain's expression, she did notice his hands fisted at his sides. She had no clue what he'd muttered, but it didn't sound at all friendly and, considering the crowd's angry reaction, it wasn't. Amid the show of raised fists and verbal condemnation, Zain turned and stormed back into the study. He didn't afford her or Deeb a passing glance, nor did he hesitate to make a swift exit, slamming the door behind him.

Madison waited for the sentries to leave before she sought confirmation or denial from her only immediate source of information. "Is it true about the baby?"

Deeb's expression remained emotionless, but she saw a flicker of concern in his eyes. "I am afraid, Miss Foster, you will have to ask the emir."

And that's exactly what Madison intended to do. First, she had to find him, and soon, before all hell broke loose.

Four

"Did you find your meal satisfactory, Your Wickedness?"

Zain looked up from his barren plate to see Maysa Barad—*Doctor* Maysa Barad—standing in the doorway wearing a bright purple caftan, her dark hair pulled back into a braid. He returned her smile, though that was the last thing he cared to do. But she was his friend, and she had opened her home to him as a temporary sanctuary. "It was very good. My compliments to your chef. He has a masterful hand."

"*She* is a master," Maysa said as she pulled back the adjacent chair and sat. "I made your dinner after I gave my chef the night off. However, since I still have household staff on the premises, we should continue to speak English to ensure our new king has his privacy."

At the moment he preferred not to be reminded of

his duty. "My position will not be official until the coronation."

"You were king the moment your father passed. My sympathies to you, though I know the two of you did not always see eye to eye."

That was an understatement. "Thank you for that, and for allowing me to arrive virtually unannounced."

"You are always welcome here, Zain." She rested her elbow on the table and supported her cheek with her palm, sending the heavy bangles at her wrists down her arm. "And you have always been the official king of mischief."

"And you are still as pretty as you were the last time I saw you."

Her smile expanded. "But are you still the little devil who attempted to frighten me with toads?"

She had been the sister he'd never had. "You were never really frightened, were you?"

"No. I was simply playing along until Rafiq came along to rescue me."

Zain had always suspected that to be the case. Maysa had been in love with his brother for as long as he could recall. He wondered if she still was. "Speaking of Rafiq, will you be attending the wedding?"

She straightened in the chair, her frame as rigid as the carved wooden table. "I received an invitation, but do not wish to witness that charade."

Yes, she was still in love with Rafiq. "I agree it might not be the best match."

"A match made in misery. Rafiq will never be happy with a woman whose heart belongs to another man."

"What man?"

Zain saw a flash of regret pass over her expression.

"I would rather not say. In fact, I have already said too much."

"Can you tell me if Rima has returned this man's affections?"

"Yes, she has."

He tried to contain his shock. "Does Rafiq know?"

She lifted her shoulders in a shrug. "If he does, he has chosen to ignore it. Regardless, it is not my place to tell him, and I would hope you keep it to yourself, as well."

He did not like the thought of concealing the truth from his brother, yet he doubted Rafiq would believe him. "It would not matter, Maysa. Rafiq is all about duty, regardless of the circumstance. He has every intention of honoring the marriage contract."

She flipped her hand in dismissal. "Enough talk about your brother and his bride. Tell me about California. I did not have the opportunity to visit there when I was in medical school in the States."

Los Angeles had only been his home base and little more. "I traveled a good deal of the time."

"Then tell me about that. I am sure you met many interesting people and saw many interesting sights."

He had seen devastation, drought, famine and disease. Sights he never cared to see again, especially in his own country. "I'm certain my experiences do not compare to yours as a physician."

She shook her head. "My experiences have been challenging since my return to Bajul. I am the only female doctor and the only one who will treat those who can pay very little, if at all. The others cater to the wealthier population."

That came as no surprise to Zain. "Your commitment is admirable, Maysa. Once I am fully in charge, I will make certain the hospital undergoes renovations and medical offices are added. Perhaps then you can receive pay for your services."

"I do not need the money as much as the people need my help," she said. "Fortunately, my father has allowed me to live in his palatial second home regardless that I have failed him as a daughter. He is also kind enough to provide the funds to keep the household going, though I despise taking even one riyal from him."

Zain could not imagine a father considering his daughter a failure after she had established a successful medical career. But then Maysa's father had always been an ass. "Does the sultan come to visit often?"

She released a bitter laugh. "Oh, no. He is either in Saudi or Yemen with my poor mother, building his fortune so that he may provide for his many mistresses."

Maysa had the same issues with her father as Zain had always had with his. "I believe I recall you were bound to a betrothal at one time. I take it that did not come to fruition."

"Actually, it did. Two weeks after the wedding, I realized that contrary to our culture, a woman does not need a man to survive. It took some effort to obtain a divorce, but I managed it. And Father has not forgiven me for it."

"I'm certain it hasn't been easy on you."

She shrugged. "I realized there would be those who would shun me because of my decision, yet I refused to let that deter me. No man will ever dictate my future."

Zain couldn't help but smile when he thought about Madison. She and Maysa were very much alike. Yet he felt more than brotherly fondness for Madison.

"Do you find me amusing, *Your Highness?*" Maysa asked.

"No. You reminded me of someone else I know."

"Someone special?"

Perhaps too special for his own good. "Actually, she is a political consultant Rafiq hired to save me from myself."

"She has a huge task ahead of her then."

"Believe me, she is up to the task. She is also very headstrong, and extremely intelligent. Fortunately, she has a sense of humor, as well. Sometimes I find her frustrating, other times extremely intriguing."

"Is she attractive?"

"Yes, but her attractiveness goes well beyond her physical appearance. She is one of the most fascinating women I have ever encountered."

She inclined her head and studied him. "You have feelings for her."

Maysa's comment took him aback. "She is an employee."

"An employee who has hypnotized you, Zain. Perhaps the sheikh has met his match in more ways than one."

"That is absurd," he said without much conviction. "I have only known her a few days."

"Yet it is those immediate connections that at times make a lasting impact on our lives."

From the wistfulness in Maysa's tone, Zain recognized she spoke from experience. "Even if I did develop these feelings you speak of, we both know a permanent relationship with an outsider could never happen."

She drummed her fingertips on the tabletop. "Ah, yes. We are back to the antiquated tradition of marrying our own kind. You have the power to change that."

"I have other changes to make that are more important. Changes that will affect the future of this country."

"And you are not concerned about your own future?" she asked. "Would you give up a chance at finding love for a tradition that should have died long ago?"

He was too tired to defend his decisions, which led to his next request. "Would you have an available room where I could stay the night?"

"I have twelve bedrooms at your disposal," she said. "But will you not be missed?"

He would, but he did not care. "Deeb knows where I am."

"Zain, although it is truly not any of my concern, you cannot hide away when times become difficult."

He tossed his napkin aside. "Then you've heard about the latest accusations."

"I was there when you spoke this morning. You had everyone in the palm of your hand until that *himar* intruded."

Zain had considered calling him something much worse than a donkey. "For your information, I am not hiding. I am only taking a brief sabbatical to gather my thoughts."

She frowned. "Forgive me for pointing this out, but you have always been one to withdraw from the world when you lose control. The role you will soon assume requires continuity. Are you certain you are willing to bear that burden?"

Though he did not appreciate her commentary, he reluctantly admitted she was partially right. "I have prepared for this opportunity for many years. Once I am established, I will commit fully to my duties."

She smiled and patted his hand. "I know you will. Now if you will follow me, I will show you to your quarters for the evening, where you can rest and fantasize about that special consultant who has obviously earned a little piece of the king's heart."

Maysa knew him all too well, yet she was wrong

about his feelings for Madison. She did not—nor would she ever—have any claim on his heart.

After Zain's twenty-four-hour absence, Madison finally located him on the palace's rooftop. He sat on the cement ground with his back against the wall, hands laced together on his belly, one long leg stretched out before him, the other bent at the knee. He seemed so lost in his thoughts, she questioned whether she should give him more alone time. Regrettably, time was a luxury they didn't have. Not when she required answers to burning questions in order to circumvent the gossip. Provided it *was* gossip.

Before moving forward, she paused a few moments to ponder his atypical clothing. The standard white tailored shirt, Italian loafers and dark slacks had been replaced by a fitted black tee, khaki cargo pants and heavy brown boots. He reminded her of an adventurous explorer ready for travel—and in some ways dressed to kill. His rugged appearance was unquestionably murdering her composure.

Madison shored up her courage, walked right up to him and hovered above him. "I see the sheikh has finally returned."

He glanced up at her, his expression somber. "How did you know where to find me?"

"Elena mentioned you might be here. She said you and your brothers used to hide from her up here when it was time for your lessons."

He smiled but it faded fast. "I should have known she would give my secrets away."

Madison wondered what other secrets he might be keeping. "Mind if I join you?"

He gestured toward the space beside him. "It's less than comfortable, but be my guest."

She carefully lowered herself to the ground and hugged her knees to her chest, taking care to make sure the hem of her dress was properly in place. "The next time you decide to do a disappearing act, do you mind letting me in on it?"

"I assure you, it will not happen again."

"I hope I can trust you on that. You wouldn't believe how frantic everyone was until Mr. Deeb told us you were safe."

"I was never in danger," he said as he continued to stare straight ahead. "I stayed with a friend at a house in the foothills."

She could only imagine what that might have entailed if that friend happened to be female. "How did you get there? And how did you manage to evade your bodyguards? Rafiq is still furious over that."

"I took one of the all-terrain vehicles, and Deeb was aware of my departure. Guards are not necessary when I take care to disguise myself."

She noticed a camouflage baseball cap resting at his side. "So that's the reason for the casual clothes?"

"They serve me well in hiding my identity."

They served him well in highlighting his finer points, and that sent her straight into a fishing expedition. "And this friend had no qualms about concealing the future king?"

"Maysa understands my need for privacy. She made certain I was not disturbed."

As she'd gathered—a woman friend. "Does this friendship come with or without benefits?" She hated that she sounded like some jealous lover.

"Without benefits," he said before adding, "although I do not expect you to believe me."

He sounded more frustrated than angry. "I never said I didn't believe you."

He sent her a sideways glance. "Then you are in the minority. Most people choose to believe the worst of me."

She lowered her legs and shifted slightly to face him. "Since it seems you don't have an official press secretary, I spent the day sending out releases stating you vehemently deny fathering Keeley Winterlind's child. The question is, did I lie?"

"No."

She released the breath she didn't know she'd been holding. "Not even a remote possibility?"

"No."

She truly wanted to believe him, but… "I do remember seeing photos of the two of you a couple years ago."

"That means nothing." Now he sounded angry.

"It means there's proof you had a connection with her."

"A platonic connection," he said. "I came upon her ex-lover threatening her at a social gathering and I intervened. We remained in contact because she needed someone to set her on the right path. However, she was young and impressionable and immature. The last I heard, she had reunited with the boyfriend because I could not convince her that the controlling bastard wasn't good for her."

If what he'd said was true, then in essence he was a champion of women. "Do you think she's the one claiming you're her baby's father?"

"No. She contacted me this afternoon and assured me she had nothing to do with the speculation, and I trust her. She also confirmed the ex is the father."

"I'm relieved I told the truth when I denied the speculation."

"As if that will do any good."

He seemed so sullen, Madison felt the need to lift his spirits. "Have you seen the news footage of your speech?"

"No, and I refuse to watch it."

No surprise there. "Well, you looked incredibly debonair and poised." And absolutely gorgeous. "I'm sure you'll start receiving requests for invitations from a slew of queen candidates."

"I highly doubt they would be interested in light of the recent attacks on my character."

Her efforts to cheer him up were on the verge of becoming an epic failure. "Hey, if they could see you in your adventurer's gear, they wouldn't care about your character."

She'd finally coaxed a smile from him. A tiny smile, but at least it was something. "I fail to understand how I could charm a woman with clothing not fit for a king."

"Then maybe you don't know women as well as you think you do. Of course, it doesn't hurt you're the ruler of a country, and your house isn't too shabby, either."

For the first time since her arrival, he gave her his full attention and a fully formed smile. "You are looking quite beautiful tonight."

She couldn't immediately recall the last time any man had called her beautiful. Her shapeless aqua sundress certainly wouldn't qualify. "Thank you, but this outfit is designed solely for comfort, not beauty."

"I was not referencing your clothing." He lightly touched her cheek. "You are beautiful."

When Madison contacted those dark, mysterious eyes, that spark of awareness threatened to become a flame. With little effort, it could blaze out of control. Yet she recognized Zain was only attempting to divert attention from the seriousness of the situation, and possibly cover his internal turmoil. She truly wanted to provide him with a diversion, but the last thing Zain needed was a potential scandal involving his political consultant. The last thing she needed was to venture into personal involvement with him. She'd already started down that slippery slope.

She shored up her wavering willpower. "Now that we have engaged in sufficient mutual admiration, we should probably go inside and discuss how we're going to handle any other problems that might arise. I'd also be happy to listen to what you have planned for the council meeting tomorrow."

"I prefer to stay here with you."

And she wanted to stay with him, honestly she did, but to what end? "If we stay much longer, we could make another mistake."

He searched her face and paused at her mouth before returning to her eyes. "I have made many mistakes in my lifetime, but spending time with you will not ever be a mistake."

Her foolish heart executed a little flip-flop in her chest. "Flattery will get you everywhere."

"Everywhere?"

One more sexy word out of his incredible mouth and she'd be too far gone to stop any madness that might occur. "The only place we should be going is into your office, and repairing your reputation is the only thing we should consider."

He studied the stars and sighed. A rough, sensuous and slightly irritated sigh. "You are right. Business should always come before pleasure, no matter how revolting that business might be."

Madison was admittedly somewhat disappointed that he conceded so quickly. "You will get through this, Zain. It's only a matter of time before you earn your country's trust. You are destined to be a great leader."

"I sincerely appreciate your faith in my abilities."

He both looked and sounded sincere, causing her spirits to rise. "Now let's get some work done before dawn."

When Zain came to his feet and held out his hand to help her up, Madison wasn't quite prepared for the sharp sting of awareness as they stood. She wasn't exactly surprised when he framed her face in his palm. But the sudden impact of his mouth covering hers nearly buckled her knees. The kiss was powerful, almost desperate, yet she didn't have the will to stop him. Every argument she'd made against this very thing went the way of the warm breeze surrounding them.

She somehow wound up backed against the wall with Zain flush against her. Even when he left her mouth to trail kisses down her neck, lowered one strap and slid the tip of his tongue slightly beneath the scoop neck of her dress, she disregarded the warning bells sounding in her head. Even when he worked her hem up to her waist, slipped his hands down the back of her panties and clasped her bottom, she couldn't manage one protest. And as he kissed her again, pressed as close to her as he possibly could and simulated the act she'd been determined to avoid with both his body and tongue, stop became go and thinking became an impossible effort.

Separated only by silk and cotton, Madison felt the beginnings of a climax, prompting an odd sound bubbling up from her throat. She was vaguely aware of the rasp of a zipper, very aware the no-return point had arrived and extremely aware when Zain abruptly let her go.

She closed her eyes and waited until her respiration had almost returned to normal before she risked a glance to see him facing the wall, both hands raised above his head as if in surrender. "It appears we're suffering from restraint issues."

He straightened and redid his fly. "Suffering is an apt description."

She pushed the strap back into place while struggling for something more to say. "Out of curiosity, why did you stop?"

He leaned back against the stone and stared straight ahead. "You deserve better than frantic sex against a wall."

"Honestly, it was the hottest few moments of my life and frankly out of character for me."

"Leave, Madison."

The command caught her off guard. "We still have to go over—"

"We'll meet in the morning."

"But you need—"

"I need you to go before I am tempted to carry you to my bed and complete your climax before giving you another while I am inside you."

Madison understood that, loud and clear. She couldn't remember ever having such a heated physical reaction to a man's words. Then again, no man had ever said anything remotely close to that to her. "I'm not leaving until I make myself clear. Whatever this thing is between us, it's going to take a lot of strength to ignore it. I'm not sure that's going to happen, so we have two options. One, we accept we're consenting adults and just do it and get it out of our system. Or I bow out gracefully before I cause you more problems."

He finally looked at her. "The second option is out. The first will not be possible until I am assured you can give me what I need."

Surely he wasn't suggesting… "Are you questioning my lovemaking abilities?"

"No. I need to know I have your respect and above all, your trust."

With that, Zain turned and disappeared through the opening leading to the stairway.

Madison sank back onto the ground and pinched the bridge of her nose from the onset of a tremendous headache. She did respect Zain and his ideals. Did she trust him? At the moment, she wasn't sure.

"My apologies for disturbing you, Emir."

Zain tossed his notes onto the side table to acknowledge Deeb, who had somehow entered his suite without his notice. But then he'd been distracted since he'd left Madison on the rooftop an hour ago. "What is it, Deeb?"

"I wanted to know if you required anything before I leave for home."

He needed the woman in the bedroom next door, but he could not have her. Not yet. "You are dismissed."

Deeb nodded and said, "Have a restful evening, Your Highness."

That was not a likely prospect. When Deeb retreated toward the door, Zain reconsidered and called him back. "I have a few questions for you." Questions he had intentionally failed to ask for fear of the answers.

Deeb pushed the glasses up on his nose. "Yes?"

Zain shifted in the less-than-comfortable chair. "How long have you been employed by the royal family?"

"Fifteen years last December."

His thoughts drifted off topic momentarily. "And you never thought to marry during that time?"

"I am married. I have been for fifteen years."

He was surprised Deeb had not mentioned that before, but then he had never inquired about his private life. "Children?"

A look of pride passed over the man's expression. "I have six children, four boys and two girls. The oldest is nine, the youngest three months."

As far as Zain was concerned, that was quite a feat for several reasons. "You were with me in the States for seven years, so I find that rather remarkable."

"If you recall, you allowed me to return to Bajul during your travels."

Clearly the man impregnated his bride every time he'd been home. "And your wife did not take exception to your absences?"

Deeb hinted at a smile. "If that were true, we would not have six children."

Zain could not argue that. "Are you still happily wed?"

"Yes, Emir."

Zain tented his fingers beneath his chin. "To what do you attribute that happiness?"

"Patience and tolerance. Most important, sustained passion. When you choose your mate, it is best to always remember this."

He could not agree more, especially when it came to the passion. "I appreciate the advice."

"You are welcome, Your Highness. Now if that is all—"

"It is not." He had to pose one more question. An extremely difficult question. "Do you know if the rumors of my father's infidelity are true?"

Deeb tugged at his collar as if he had a noose around his neck. "I feel compelled not to betray the king's confidence."

As suspected, he did have information. "You need not conceal my father's secrets any longer, Deeb. You answer to me now." He despised sounding so harsh, but he was that desperate for confirmation.

"I know of only one woman," he said after a brief hesitation.

"Who is this woman?"

"I will only say that she is above reproach. She was only doing the king's bidding."

Zain sensed that Deeb was protecting more than the king's secrets. He could very well have a connection with the mistress, which led him to believe she could have been a former staff member. At the moment, he was too exhausted to press his assistant for more details. "That will be all, Deeb."

"As you wish." Deeb turned to leave before facing Zain again. "If I may speak candidly, I would like to add that some things are not as they seem."

He'd said that to Madison on more than one occasion. "Perhaps, yet you cannot deny that my father dishonored my mother?"

"Again, every situation is unique and at times not for us to judge."

Zain could not help but judge his father. The man had caused him to doubt himself on many levels, the least of which had to do with personal relationships. "Thank you for your candor. You may go now."

"Before I take my leave," he said, "may I speak freely?"

"You may." For now.

"If it is any solace, I firmly believe you are nothing like the king."

With that, Deeb left the room, leaving Zain in a state of disbelief. He learned tonight how little he knew about his assistant, yet the man seemed to know much about him.

Feeling restless, Zain paced the room for a few moments, growing angrier by the minute as he thought back to Deeb's confirmation of his father's infidelity. He strode to the shelf housing several books, picked up the photo of the king posing with a U.S. president and hurled it against the far wall. The glass shattered and rained down in shards to the carpeted floor.

Despite Deeb's insistence there were extenuating circumstances, Zain could never forgive his father. Not when his ruthless behavior had dealt his mother the worst fate. Death.

Five

The second she walked into the conference room, Madison felt as if she'd entered Antarctica. With their immaculate black suits and impeccable grooming, Rafiq and Zain Mehdi could be corporate raiders involved in a business debate, not two brothers engaged in an ongoing war of wills.

"Good afternoon, gentlemen," she said as she pulled out a chair across from Zain, sat and scooted beneath the massive conference table.

"Do you have anything to report on the latest scandal?" Rafiq asked, while Zain seemed more interested in the view out the window at Madison's back.

She set her briefcase at her feet and folded her hands on the table. "I do, actually." A report that wouldn't go over well with Zain. "I spent most of the morning on the phone tracking down Ms. Winterlind's publicist. I finally heard from her a few moments ago."

Zain finally looked at her when she hesitated. "And?"

"She told me that Ms. Winterlind did in fact leak the initial claim that you're the father of her baby."

Anger flashed in Zain's eyes. "Impossible."

"I'm afraid it's not. She did send her apologies to you through the publicist and is in the process of retracting the claim."

"It seems your faith in the model was misplaced, Zain," Rafiq said.

If looks really could kill, Zain had just delivered a visual bullet, right between his brother's eyes. "She had her reasons."

"What would those be, brother? She has her sights set on trapping a king?"

Zain muttered something acid and probably insulting in Arabic. "She is not like that, Rafiq."

Time for a much-needed intervention on Zain's behalf. "Actually, Prince Rafiq, she made the claim to protect her son from her ex, who is a known batterer. Fortunately, he's currently incarcerated on assault charges."

Zain's gaze snapped to hers. "Did he beat her?"

Evidently he still cared about the model, maybe even more than he'd let on in their previous conversations. "No. He beat up some guy in a bar and nearly killed him. He'll be going away for a long time."

"Good riddance," Zain muttered.

"Are there other women who will surface with similar claims?" Rafiq asked Zain, venom in his tone.

Zain's eyes narrowed. "The women with whom I have been intimately involved are trustworthy."

"I believe the model contradicts that assertion."

"I was not intimate with her."

Rafiq raised a brow. "Then it would seem those whom

you have bedded and spurned would be more likely to lie."

Zain looked as if he might bolt out of the chair. *"Izhab ila al djaheem, Rafiq."*

Madison had no idea what Zain had said to his brother, but she did feel she needed to defuse the situation, possibly at her own peril. "Look, Your Highness, Prince Rafiq does have a point. We need to know if there is even a remote possibility a woman might come forward with some scandalous claim, unfounded or not."

Zain's expression turned cold. "My former lovers should not be a concern, unless perhaps one is interested in the extent of my sexual experience."

His attitude, and the pointed comment, shredded her already thinned patience. "I don't need a list, only a number. Less than five? More than ten? Fifty?" Now *she* sounded like a scorned lover.

"I assure you, my past will not affect my ability to lead," he said. "Many married leaders worldwide have openly engaged in affairs and continued to rule."

Madison had known more than her fair share. Some came through it unscathed. Others had not. "Any scandal could influence your people's trust in you if it rears its ugly head again."

He kept his gaze centered on hers. "Does that include your trust in me, Madison?"

"Trust is earned, *Zain*."

She regretted the informality faux pas the minute she glanced at Rafiq and saw the suspicious look in his eyes. She could only imagine how the exchange sounded— like lovers engaged in a spat.

Rafiq checked his watch and stood. "The meeting begins in ten minutes. You can continue this discussion later."

Madison might receive an emphatic no, but she had to ask. "I'd like to sit in on the meeting."

Rafiq looked as though she'd requested to run naked through the royal gardens. "That is not permitted."

"I will allow it," Zain said. "You may observe from the gallery. I'll have Deeb interpret for you."

She wasn't sure if Zain had granted her request because he wanted her there, or because he wanted to one-up his brother. It didn't matter as long as she had a ringside seat where she could watch him in action.

When Zain failed to stand, Rafiq nailed him with another glare. "Are you coming now, or should I have the guards escort you?"

"I will be along shortly," Zain said. "I need to speak privately with Ms. Foster."

"I have no doubt you do." With that, Rafiq strode out of the room.

As soon as the door closed, Madison directed her attention to Zain. "This is exactly what I feared would happen. My stupid miscue with your name wasn't lost on your brother. There's no telling what he thinks is going on between us."

"Let him believe what he will," he said. "He would have assumed the worst whether I had touched you or not."

Oh, but he had touched her. "If you're not concerned about Rafiq, then why did you need to speak to me in private?"

He looked all too serious. "First, I want to apologize. My problem is with Rafiq's attitude, not yours. Second, I need to know if you're all right after last evening."

She shrugged. "I'm fine. It happened, it's done and it's over."

He inclined his head and studied her. "Is it truly over?"

If only she could say yes without any reservations. Trouble was, she couldn't. "Right now you need to concentrate on what you have to propose to the council."

He reached across the table and took her hand. "How can I concentrate when I know you're upset?"

"I told you, I'm fine." She came to her feet and grabbed her briefcase. "I'm sure you'll regain your full concentration once you're in the meeting. Now let's go before Rafiq calls out the guard."

As Zain stood, Madison started toward the door. But before she made it more than a few steps, Zain caught her arm and turned her to face him. "Do you recall what I said to you last night?"

She recalled every detail of last night. "Yes, and I meant what I said to you a few minutes ago. You're going to have to prove you're trustworthy."

"At times trust requires a leap of faith."

If she leaped too quickly, she could land in an emotional briar patch. "Faith has failed me before."

"You are not alone in that. Yet whatever my faults might be, I am a man of my word."

She really wanted to believe that. "Speaking of words, you've never told me what you said to me the day you addressed the crowd."

He rubbed his thumb slowly back and forth down her arm. Not only could she feel it through her linen jacket, she could feel it everywhere. "You really wish for me to tell you now?"

"Yes, I do." Although she had a feeling she might regret it.

As he had the first time he'd whispered words she

hadn't understood, he rested his lips against her ear. "You should never have kissed me."

He had to be kidding. "That's it? You're saying the kiss was all my fault?"

"No. It was my fault for baiting you. I simply did not believe you would take the bait. However, if we had never shared that first kiss, I would not be lying awake at night fantasizing about all the ways I would make love to you. I would not want you so badly that I would gladly reschedule this meeting and take you away from here."

He released her then, walked to the door and left the room, while she stood still as a statue, cursing Zain for his uncanny knack of keeping her off balance. She didn't move an inch until Deeb summoned her into the hallway.

Madison followed the entourage down the corridor, watching as Zain walked ahead with overt confidence. Several times she had to tear her gaze away after trying to sneak a peek at his notable royal butt. Once they reached the end of the hall, Zain walked through double doors while Deeb showed Madison to his right, where they descended a short flight of stairs, and into the glass-enclosed gallery.

Madison took a seat in the front row of chairs beside him and looked down on the scene. Several men were seated at a large round table—eleven by her count—all dressed in high-neck button-down white robes, various colored sashes draped around their necks, and white kaffiyehs with bands that matched the sashes. The chairs flanking either side of Rafiq were noticeably empty, one most likely reserved for Zain. She leaned toward Deeb and asked, "Who's missing, aside from His Highness?"

"The youngest emir, Adan," he said. "He is excused today due to the importance of his mission."

Madison doubted Zain would be afforded the same

courtesy if he'd decided not to appear. As the minutes ticked off, she began to worry he might have taken that route. And considering the way the council members kept looking around, she assumed they were worried, as well.

A few seconds later, the doors opened to the future king, prompting the men to stand. He wore the same white robe with a gold-and-black sash draped around his neck, but nothing on his head. She didn't know if he was intentionally bucking tradition, or if someone had forgotten his headdress. Frankly, that was fine by Madison. She'd hate to see even one inch of that pretty face concealed from her view.

When Zain lowered himself into the chair, the men followed suit while Deeb reached forward and flipped a switch to the intercom. Zain began to speak in a language that Madison regretted not learning. She'd only mastered a few official greetings and the all-important request for the ladies' room. Perhaps she would ask Zain to teach her more. She imagined he could teach her quite a bit from a nonlinguistic standpoint, and she would happily be a willing student.

Madison forced her attention back to the meeting and wondered what she'd hoped to gain by observing when she couldn't understand a word.

Deeb demonstrated that he understood her confusion when he said, "They are currently discussing economic concerns. Rafiq is the minister of finance."

"And Adan?" she asked.

"He is the head of the military."

That made sense. Unfortunately, nothing else did.

As the discourse continued, Madison became focused on watching Zain's hands move as he spoke. Strong, steady, expressive hands. Skilled hands. Her thoughts drifted back to the night before when she'd experienced those hands on her body. She'd wanted to experience more of them in places that he'd obviously avoided. The sudden, unexpected rush of heat caused her to cross her legs against the sensations. She felt as she might actually start to squirm if she didn't get her mind back on business. Easier said than done.

Hormone overload, pure and simple. What else could it possibly be?

You've never been so attuned to someone that when you enter a room, that person is all you see? You've never wanted someone so desperately that you would risk everything to have them?

Yes, she wanted Zain, with a force that defied logic. Even more now after what he'd said only minutes ago.

I would not be lying awake at night fantasizing about all the ways I would make love to you.

Graphic, detailed images of making love with Zain filtered into Madison's mind when she should have been focusing on the meeting. She shifted her crossed legs from restlessness and pure, undeniable desire for a man who shouldn't be on her sexual radar. But he was, front and center, sending out signals that she urgently wanted to answer.

The sound of raised voices jarred Madison out of her fantasies and back into reality. She regarded Deeb, who appeared impervious to the disruption.

"What's happening now?" she asked.

"The emir is explaining his water proposal. Sheikh Barad has taken exception to it."

"Which one is he?"

"To the right of Prince Rafiq."

Madison honed in on a fierce-looking man with a neatly trimmed goatee and beady eyes. "Is he a relative?"

"No. He is a childhood friend of Prince Rafiq's. His sister, Maysa, is a physician."

Maysa. The woman Zain had visited the other night. "He doesn't appear to care for Zain."

"He does not care for the emir's plan, nor does he care for the emir's demand that he halt any plans for drilling."

Obviously oil and water truly didn't mix in this case. "Is this going to be a problem for Zain?" Not again. "His Highness?"

Deeb didn't seem at all disturbed by her second informality screwup. "That depends on how he chooses to handle the matter."

Zain chose to handle it by rising from the chair and slamming his palm on the table. He then launched into an impassioned diatribe that seemed to silence everyone into submission.

"He is telling everyone that he is the king," Deeb began. "His word is the law, and those who go against him will be summarily dismissed and tried for treason."

Apparently Zain was dead serious. "What does that entail?"

"If found guilty, a firing squad."

Madison wondered if that held true for unsuitable women who overstepped their bounds and slept with the king. She preferred not to find out.

Zain reclaimed his seat but continued to speak, this time in low, more temperate tones. Deeb explained that he spoke of the people, their needs and the importance of their future, the evils of profiteering and raping the land, as well as his commitment to bringing the country into the twenty-first century. "If there are those who do not support his vision," Deeb continued, "they may relinquish their positions immediately."

As Zain continued to address the men, Madison found

his absolute control, his sheer air of power, as heady as a hot bath. Funny, she had never been turned on by authoritative men. Then again, she'd never met anyone like Zain before. Not even close. In the five years she'd lived with her former boyfriend, not once had Jay ever made her feel as if she might climb out of her skin if she didn't have him. Not once did she spot him across a crowded room and feel an overwhelming sense of passion.

Without warning, Zain abruptly stood, did an about-face and strode out of the room, leaving the men exchanging glances with each other, their mouths agape. Everyone but Rafiq, who looked more angry than shocked.

"I guess the meeting's over," Madison said as the rest of the members began to exit, one by one.

"Yes, it is," Deeb said solemnly. "Unfortunately, the emir's problems have only begun."

Madison understood that all too well. Her respect for Zain had risen tenfold, but so had the realization that his position required his undivided attention. He couldn't afford any distractions, and that included her.

Feeling a headache coming on, Madison left the gallery and headed straight for her quarters. She vowed that from this point forward, she would avoid being alone with Zain.

"I must commend you on your success, brother."

With only a brief glance at Rafiq standing at the study door, Zain tossed the robe onto the sofa and claimed the place beside it. "I am pleased you have finally realized I am quite capable of handling my duties."

Rafiq strolled into the room and took the opposing chair. "I am not referring to your duty. I am referring to Ms. Foster. It has taken you less than five days to bed her. However, that is still two days more than the new cook's assistant ten years ago."

He should have known his sibling would never congratulate him on his success with the council meeting. "And if my memory serves me correctly, you slept with the gardener's daughter the day you met her, brother."

Rafiq presented an acerbic smile. "True, but that young woman did not have the power to destroy my reputation."

"Neither does Ms. Foster, and for your information, I have not slept with her." Not beyond his fantasies.

"All signs point to the contrary."

"And your imagination is out of control."

"I did not imagine the way the two of you looked at each other earlier today," Rafiq said. "Nor did I imagine your talk of trust."

"She was referring to trust in regard to my recent disappearance." Only a partial truth. "You always have, and always will, assume that I have no self-control when it comes to the opposite sex."

"I would be joined by the rest of the world in that assumption."

With effort, Zain kept his anger in check. "Perhaps that is why you hired Ms. Foster. You were setting me up to fail because of the temptation she poses."

He presented a self-satisfied smile. "Then you admit you are tempted by her."

More than his brother knew. "And you are not?"

"I am to be married in two weeks' time."

"You are still a man, Rafiq, and you are marrying a woman who does not support your libido, only your foreign bank account."

Rafiq came to his feet. "I have no time for this. But mark my words, should you give in to temptation with

Ms. Foster, you are taking a risk that could destroy what little standing you have left among our people."

Zain refused to comment as his brother exited the room. Yes, Madison posed a tremendous temptation. And yes, any intimacy with her would come with considerable risk. But she had become one of his greatest weaknesses in the past few days. Perhaps one of his greatest weaknesses ever.

Feeling restless and ready to run, Zain decided he needed some space. He knew exactly where he wanted to go, and he did not intend to go alone.

"Change into some comfortable clothes and shoes, and come with me."

Madison remained at the open veranda door, determined to stand her ground with Zain. "After today, running off together is the last thing you need. In fact, I've decided it's best we aren't alone together again."

"We will not be alone for long on this journey."

Evidently they'd be accompanied by a contingent of guards, which would be for the best—if she decided to go with him. "Where exactly do you plan to take me?"

"It's a surprise."

She planted her fists on her hips and refused to budge. "I'm not too fond of surprises."

He leaned a shoulder against the doorframe. "You will enjoy this one. We do need to hurry to reach our destination on time."

"Which is?"

"On the outskirts of the village. It will take us a while to arrive there."

Could he be any more vague? "As far as I know, the village is only a mile or so from the palace, which is about a two minute drive. Are we going by camel?"

He had the gall to grin. "No. We are going by foot."

He'd evidently lost his royal mind if he honestly believed she'd agree to traipse down a mountain in the dark. She was basically a klutz on level ground in broad daylight. "You're proposing we walk down to the village at dusk."

"Yes, and if you will stop talking and start dressing, we might be there before dawn."

He apparently wouldn't give up until she gave in, and she wasn't quite ready to do that. "I refuse to go unless you give me details."

He streaked a hand over his chin. "All right. I want you to see the village with me serving as your guide. I want you to know the people and understand why my position as their king holds great importance."

"Why didn't you just say that in the first place?"

"Because you are quite beautiful when you are not in control."

And he was quite the cad. An incredibly sensual cad. "I'll go, but only on one condition."

He released a rough sigh. "What would that be?"

"You say please."

He took her hand and gave it a light kiss. "Would you please do me the honor of allowing me to show you my world?"

How could she refuse him now? "Fine. Just give me a few minutes."

"Wear a waterproof jacket, since rain is predicted for later tonight."

Great. "You expect me to walk back up the mountain in the dark all wet?"

He grinned. "There is no guarantee you will be wet, but chances are you very well could be, whether it rains or not."

The innuendo wasn't lost on Madison, or her contrary libido. "If you don't behave, I'm staying here."

His smile faded into a frown. "I will arrange transportation for our return if that will satisfy you."

"That will." She could only hope he made good on his word. "Wait here while I change."

"I may not come inside and wait?"

How easy it would be to say yes, but if she did, they might forgo their little expedition for a different kind of journey. In bed. "No, you may not wait inside."

"You still do not trust me."

"Not when my underwear happens to be involved."

After closing the door on him, Madison piled her hair into a ponytail then quickly changed into a T-shirt, jeans, her lone pair of sneakers and an all-weather lightweight coat. Probably not the best in the way of hiking clothes, but they'd have to do.

She returned to the veranda to find him leaning back against the wall, a military-green jacket covering his black tee and beige cargo pants, the camouflage baseball cap set low on his brow. For all intents and purposes, he could be an ordinary man on a mission of leisure. Yet there was nothing ordinary about those pensive dark eyes.

He held out his hand to her. "Are you ready for an adventure?"

That depended on what kind of adventure he had in mind. Only one way to find out. "As ready as I'll ever be."

After Madison clasped his offered hand, Zain led her down the side stairs leading to the labyrinth of courtyards on the ground level. He came to a small iron gate and opened it to a rock path that led away from the rear of the palace. The stone soon turned to dirt, and the trail soon took a sharp downward descent.

"Are you sure this is safe?" she asked when they reached a rocky place that looked way too precarious to go forward.

Zain released her, stepped down and then signaled her forward. "Take my hand and I'll assist you."

She would rather ride down on his back but that could be a bit awkward. "Okay, if you say so."

Slowly, steadily, they navigated the pathway until they finally reached firm footing, and not once had Zain let her go. She began to relax as they continued on, knowing he would do his best to keep her out of harm's way. But then he came to an ominous-looking boulder pile and started to climb.

"Follow me," he said over one shoulder.

Madison remained at the bottom and glared up at him. "Excuse me, but I thought we're supposed to be going down, not up."

"First, you must see the view from here before we continue."

Her gaze wandered up to the plateau. "You can describe it to me."

"You have to witness it firsthand."

"I can't see it if I break my neck."

He scurried down and gestured toward the formation. "I will be immediately behind you offering support should you need it. Trust me, I will not let you fall."

She did trust him, at least in this case. "Okay, I'll do it, as long as you keep your eye on the goal and not on my butt."

He smiled. "I cannot promise I will not look, but I will try to refrain from touching you."

And she'd try to refrain from requesting he touch her, though she couldn't promise that, either.

One foot in front of the other, she silently chanted as

she began the ascent. Truth was, she'd hiked before in similar terrain, just not in a long time. Yet her confidence grew knowing Zain would catch her if she stumbled. And with only moderate effort, she made it to the top just in time to catch the view of the valley washed in the final rays of the setting sun.

"Unbelievable," she muttered when Zain came up behind her. "I can see so much more here than on the veranda."

"I told you it was not to be missed." He rested his hands lightly on her shoulders. "If you look closely, you can see the lake right beyond the base of Mabrúruk."

She spotted a patch of cerulean-blue on the horizon. "I see it. Is that a hotel on the cliff above it?"

"A resort," he said. "It's owned by the Barad family and managed by Shamil Barad."

"Maysa's brother," Madison replied. "Mr. Deeb told me about him."

"Maysa is nothing like him." He sounded and looked irate. "Where she cares about the people, Shamil only cares about padding his fortune at any cost."

"Believe me, I've met his kind. And I'm positive you'll keep him in his place."

He leaned and kissed her cheek. "I truly appreciate your confidence in me."

As Zain continued to point out the landmarks, Madison found herself leaning back against him. And when he slipped his arms around her waist, she didn't bother to pull away. She simply marveled at the passion in his voice when he spoke about his people, and relished the way he made her felt so protected.

A span of silence passed before Madison looked up at him. "You really love your country, don't you?"

"Yes, I do," he said as he stared off into the distance.

"That is why I cannot fail, yet the burden to succeed at times seems too heavy for one man to bear. Especially a flawed man like myself."

She sensed making that admission had cost him, and that alone made her appreciate him all the more. She turned into his arms and gave him a smile. "But you will succeed, Zain. You have too much conviction not to see this through."

"I am certainly going to try." For a moment he looked as though he might kiss her but surprisingly let her go. "We'd best be on our way, otherwise we will be walking in the dark."

"If we must."

Zain led the way, his hand firmly gripping hers as they made their way down the slope. Once at the bottom, he took her by the waist, lifted her up and set her on her feet. "I am so glad I made it without breaking something," she said as she tightened the band securing her hair.

"I would never let you fall, Madison."

Oh, but she was in the process of falling for him, and he couldn't be her human safety net. In a matter of weeks, she would leave him behind, and she'd have only the memories of a man who was beginning to mean too much to her. So tonight, she would make more good memories that would remain long after they'd said goodbye.

Six

"How much farther is it?"

Zain glanced back at Madison, who was trudging up the drive slowly. "Only thirty meters or so."

"My metrics suck, Zain," she said, sounding winded. "And apparently so does my stamina. But at least you were kind enough to stop for food, however rushed the meal might have been."

He'd feared being identified in such a public place. Fortunately, they'd somehow escaped recognition. "We are almost there."

As they rounded the bend, the three-quarter moon provided enough light to illuminate the small flat-roofed structure that had been a second home during his youth. He paused and pointed. "It is right there."

She came to his side and squinted. "Who lives here?"

"My friend Malik. He owns the surrounding land and raises sheep."

Madison knelt to retie her shoe. "Does he know we're coming?"

"No, but he will be glad to see me." Or so he hoped. Seven years had come and gone since their last contact, but they had been the best of friends though they lived on opposite sides of the social dividing line.

She straightened and secured the band in her hair. "Let's get going, then, before my legs give out completely. If that happens, you'll have to carry me the rest of the way."

He saw no reason not to do that now. Without giving Madison warning, he swept her up, tossed her over his shoulder and started toward their destination.

"Put me down, you royal caveman."

Had she not been laughing, he would have complied due to the insult. "I am not a caveman. I am a gentleman."

"A gentleman Neanderthal."

"I am the Neanderthal who is coming to your rescue, therefore you should refrain from complaining."

"My hero."

Ignoring her sarcasm, he continued until he made it up the single step and onto the small porch before he slid her down to her feet. "Are you sufficiently rested now?"

She adjusted her clothing and sighed. "I'm probably a mess."

"You are a beautiful mess."

She smiled. "You are a wonderful liar."

He reached out and touched her flushed cheek. "It is unfortunate you do not realize the extent of your beauty, yet is it also refreshing. I have known too many women whose beauty is only superficial. Yours is far-reaching."

She laid her palm on his hand. "You are determined to say all the right things tonight, aren't you?"

He also wanted to do all the right things, avoiding any missteps along the way. That alone prevented him from kissing her now, though he desperately wanted to do that, and more. "I am only trying to give you an enjoyable evening."

"So far, so good, expect for the marathon walk. Now, do you think you might want to knock before your friend goes to bed?"

"That is probably a good idea." He reluctantly dropped his hand from her face and rapped on the door.

Several minutes passed before Malik answered the summons. "Yes?"

Zain removed his cap. "Do you have water for two weary travelers, *sadiq?*"

The initial confusion on his friend's face quickly dissolved into recognition. "Zain, is that you?"

"Have I changed that much?"

Malik greeted him with a stern expression. "No, you have not changed. You are still the *kalet* who always appears unannounced."

Sadly, he had mistakenly believed he would be welcome. "Perhaps I should return another time."

"I prefer not to wait another seven years before I can beat you at a game of Tarneeb." He opened the door wide and grinned. *"Marhaban, sadiq."*

The warm greeting lifted Zain's spirits and concerns. He entered the house and accepted his friend's brief embrace before he remembered Madison was still waiting outside.

He turned and gestured her forward. "Malik, this is Madison Foster. Madison, Malik El-Amin."

"It's a pleasure to meet you, Malik," Madison said as she offered her hand to Malik to shake.

"Come and sit." Malik gestured toward the familiar low corner sofa covered in heavy blue fabric.

Before they could comply, a dark-haired child bolted into the room and immediately hid behind Malik. She smiled up at Zain as she twirled a long braid and rocked back and forth on her heels.

"Who have we here?" Zain asked.

"This is Lailah," Malik said as he nudged her forward. "She is six and our oldest."

"She's beautiful," Madison said from behind Zain.

Malik smiled with pride as he swept Lailah into his arms. "She fortunately resembles her mother, as do the rest of our daughters."

When a sudden, bittersweet memory filtered into Zain's mind, he pushed it aside. Yet he couldn't quite dismiss the regrets over losing touch with his friend. "How many children do you have?"

"Three more," Malik said as he set Lailah on her feet, prompting her to exit as quickly as she'd come into the room. "Badia is five and Jada is four. Ma'ali is our youngest. She arrived three months ago."

Zain patted his back. "Congratulations. It appears Mabrúuk has been good to you."

Malik frowned. "Perhaps too good."

He looked around for signs of his friend's wife. "Is Helene so exhausted she has already retired for the evening?"

"She is putting the baby to bed."

"Unfortunately, I have not been successful in that endeavor."

Zain turned his attention to the former Helene Christos, who breezed into the room, her thick brown hair flowing over her shoulders, a swaddled infant nestled in the crook of her arm. He immediately went to her and kissed both her cheeks. "You have not changed since the day you wed Malik." A somewhat controversial wedding between an Arabic farmer and a Greek-American restaurant owner's daughter. Clearly they had survived that controversy.

She frowned. "And you are forever the royal charmer, Zain Mehdi. But then I suppose I should be calling you King now. Forgive me for not bowing. I have my hands full."

He decided not to point out he was not the official king yet. "Clearly Malik has his hands full as well, since you have given him four daughters. I suppose he deserves that much."

She patted his cheek. "As do you. I wish for you many daughters and much grief protecting them from rogues like you and Malik."

"I'll second that," Madison added.

Zain felt bad for not including Madison in the conversation. Without thought, he took her hand, pulled her forward and kept his palm against the small of her back. "This is Madison Foster."

Helene eyed her for a few moments before she handed the sleeping infant over to her husband. "Are you a souvenir Zain brought from Los Angeles?"

Madison shook her head. "Not hardly. I'm currently serving as a consultant during his transition from prince to king."

"Helene's family owns the restaurant where we dined tonight," Zain added.

"The tapas were wonderful," Madison said. "I haven't found anything remotely as good in the D.C. area."

Helene's expression brightened. "You're from D.C.? My family is originally from Baltimore, although I haven't lived there since my father saw an opportunity and opened his restaurant here fifteen years ago." She reclaimed the baby from Malik before gesturing toward the sofa. "Have a seat and tell me what's the latest in spring fashion in America."

When the women settled onto the sofa to converse, Malik nodded to his right. "Let us escape before we are asked our opinions on footwear."

Zain followed Malik into the modest kitchen that had been fitted with modern appliances. "I see you have made some improvements."

Malik leaned back against the counter and folded his arms. "After my mother passed four years ago, I felt the need to make Helene feel more welcome in our home."

"I was not aware of your loss." A loss to which Zain could relate. "My sympathies. She was a good woman."

"She was a hard-working woman. She was forced to be the sole support following my father's death. I do not wish Helene to endure such hardship if I can prevent it."

Yet Malik had turned down Zain's loan offer several years ago. "Is the farming going well?"

"It has been for the last few years. After I married Helene, we were shunned by a few traditionalists but fortunately accepted by those who have blended, multicultural families. Those people kept us afloat until we finally gained acceptance."

He felt a measure of guilt that he hadn't been around to offer moral support. "I am sorry it's been so difficult for the two of you, Malik. My wish is for your continued success and a prosperous future for your family."

"You can assist us with that, Zain."

Finally, the man would let go of his pride and accept help. "How much money do you need?"

"I am not speaking of money," Malik said. "The local madrasa is in great need of funds for supplies and books. We cannot afford a private school and we want our daughters to have the best education."

Only one more change he would need to make among many. "Consider it done. I will add that to the budget now under consideration." And hoped he would not face another battle with the council.

"I appreciate whatever you can do." Malik inclined his head and sent him a curious look. "What is your true relationship with this Madison Foster?"

That happened to be one question he wasn't prepared to answer, perhaps because he was still uncertain. "As we previously explained, she is a contracted employee."

"Is serving as your lover one of the requirements?"

The question took Zain aback. "She is not my lover."

"Yet that is precisely what you are wishing for, *sadiq*."

"I did not say that." He sounded too defensive to support a denial.

Zain was certain Malik saw through his guise after his friend laid a hand on his shoulder. "When you escaped the palace to play with the local boys in the village streets on the day we met, I recognized you were destined for greatness. And when you became the chosen successor to the throne, I knew that would come to pass. Are you willing to give up your destiny for a woman who would not be deemed suitable?"

Zain tamped down his anger for the sake of friendship. "Are those not the words of a hypocrite, Malik? You did not let suitability sway you when you chose Helene."

"Yet I am not the king with an entire country following my every move."

He reluctantly acknowledged his friend had a point. "The people of this country should not be allowed to dictate my personal life or who I choose to be with."

Malik narrowed his eyes. "It is apparent this woman

means more to you than another conquest to add to all the others."

He felt the need to be truthful. "I am not certain what she means to me. I do know she seems to understand me in ways no one has before. When she's not in my presence, she is constantly in my thoughts. When I am with her, I dread the moment she has to leave me. Have you felt as if you had known someone your entire life, yet you've only known them for a few days?"

"Yes. Helene. And you, *sadiq,* are in the throes of love."

He had to believe that his current state was only the result of unrequited lust. "I cannot afford those emotions, Malik. I do know I can only consider the time we have now before she returns to America."

"And when will that be?"

"Following the coronation." The time had come to pose a request, one his friend could adamantly refuse. "Do you have a vehicle I could borrow for the evening? I will see that it is returned to you tomorrow morning."

"You did not arrive in an official car?" Malik asked.

"We walked into the village so that Madison could see the sights. Tonight I desire to be only a man with no responsibility other than being with a remarkable woman."

His friend scowled. "Yet you are a king with no car and obviously no guards."

"I do not need guards where I have been, or where I am going."

"Where would that be?"

"I wish to show Madison the lake."

Malik gave him a good-natured grin. "You wish to show her more than that, I fear. Perhaps you need protection not from guards, but from the powers of Mabrúruk."

"I only need a vehicle." In terms of lovemaking, the

protection issue would warrant discussion only if the situation arose once he had Madison alone. "Will you accommodate me, or will I need to go door-to-door to make the request?"

Malik walked to the back entrance, took a key hanging from the hook on the wall and returned to offer it to Zain. "This is to my truck. It is old and it has no rear seating, but it runs and it does have fuel, as well as two blankets for your comfort. Please return it in the same condition."

Zain pocketed the keys. "I am eternally in your debt."

"You may repay me by proceeding with caution. But then you have always been the master of escape, which leads me to believe you have a plan."

He planned only to leave as soon as possible before he had to endure more of his friend's counsel. "If you are finished with the advice, we need to be going before the night is over."

"I only have a few more words to say." When Zain opened his mouth to protest, Malik held up a hand to silence him and continued. "I understand your need to hurry, but I urge you to think before you head down the path of no return. And after some consideration, you may keep the blankets as a memento."

They shared in a hearty laugh as they returned to the living area to find the women still engaged in conversation. Zain was surprised to see Madison holding the baby against her shoulder and rocking slowly, back and forth.

She seemed very natural with the child, yet he saw a hint of sadness in her eyes when she glanced at him, and perhaps longing. That telling sign led Zain to believe she had not been honest when she'd firmly stated she had no interest in having a family. Perhaps she had not found the right man to father her children. He could be that man.

The thought came to him clear and concise, rendering him mentally off balance. He could not wish for the unattainable. He would not subject her to years of regret by wanting more from her than he could give her. But he could give her this night. A night she would not soon forget.

"Are you sure this thing is going to make it?" When Madison failed to receive a response from Zain, who had his eyes trained on the treacherous road, she gave up trying to talk to him. Between the vehicle's squeaks and groans, and the whistling wind, which had picked up steam, conversation was out of the question.

She'd climbed into the monstrosity on the assumption they were returning to the palace. She soon realized she'd been wrong when they headed away from the village and started toward the massive mountain.

Madison gripped the top of the windowless door as Zain guided the truck on a downward trek through a narrow passage comprised of boulders on both sides. She decided in this case ignorance was truly bliss and closed her eyes. She stayed that way until they came to a teeth-jarring stop.

The moon and the headlights provided enough illumination for her to view the shimmering lake spread out before them. Zain rounded the car, opened the passenger door, held out his hand and helped her climb down.

"So this is it?" she said as soon as she had her feet on solid ground. "I just wish I could see it better."

"I promised to bring you here before your departure, and with the upcoming chaos, I felt tonight would be the best time."

She didn't want to think about leaving Bajul, about

leaving him, so she wouldn't. "I'm glad we survived the drive so I could see it." Or see as much as she could.

She did spot a path leading to the shore, and immediately saw relief for her aching feet. Without another word, she took off toward the lake and, after arriving on the sandy beach, toed out of her sneakers and socks and rolled up her jeans. The minute her toes hit the cool water, she sighed at the sensations. A soothing balm for her sore soles.

"Take care of the piranha."

Madison spun around and did a little dance out of the water. When she heard the sound of Zain's laughter echoing over the area, she glanced up to see him standing above her. She considered sending him a dirty look but doubted he could see it, so she chose to give him a verbal lashing. "That was not funny at all, Zain Mehdi. It's bad enough that you took me on a dangerous joyride to get here, and now you're trying to scare me with killer fish."

He slipped his hands in his pockets. "My apologies for frightening you."

She snatched up her shoes and started toward him. "I take it there are no flesh-eating fish?"

"There are fish, but they do not crave flesh."

"Good to know, after the fact," she said when she reached him. "What now? Midnight scuba diving? Underwater basket-weaving?"

"Whatever you wish to do."

What Madison wanted to do and what she should do were two different animals. She stared up at the mist that had formed over the looming mountain, and the clouds gathering in the distance. "Since it looks like it's about to rain, we should probably head back to the palace."

"Are you afraid of rain?"

She turned her attention to Zain, specifically his eyes, which seemed darker than midnight. "I'm afraid of what might happen if we stay."

"You fear we'll make love."

"Yes, I do. I told myself I wouldn't be alone with you where anything was possible. And here we are."

He moved a little closer. "And I have told you I have certain conditions before that will happen."

"You want me to say I trust you." And if she didn't, that would be the end of it.

"Do you trust that I would never hurt you?"

Not physically, but he could hurt her in so many other ways. "I know that."

"Do you trust that what has been said about my relationships with women is not the truth?"

"Do I think your sexual exploits are overblown? Probably." Though she wasn't sure how exaggerated they might have been.

He reached out and touched her face. "Most important, you may trust that whatever happens between us tonight, I will not take it lightly. And I will not tell a soul. I only want to prove that you are a desirable, sensual woman. With that said, do you trust me?"

Call it instinct, call it crazy, but she did. "Yes, I do trust you. I'm not sure I trust myself around you."

He took her shoes, dropped them on the ground, slid her jacket away and tossed it down to join her sneakers. "I will teach you to trust your own sexuality." He shrugged out of his jacket and added it to the pile. "I only ask that you let go of your inhibitions."

That could be a test for her normally cautious self, and she wondered if going forward would be worth the risk. Yet when he pulled her into his arms and lowered his mouth to hers, she began to believe she could meet the challenge. He kissed her gently at first, just a light tease of his tongue against hers. Then he held her tighter, kissed her deeply, thoroughly, until her pulse started to sprint. The rain had begun to lightly fall, but she didn't care. Didn't care that before this was over, she would be soaked to the skin. Come to think of it, they could be down to only skin very, very soon.

Madison started to protest when Zain pulled away and stepped back. But all arguments died on her lips as he tugged his shirt over his head and tossed it aside. Due to the limited light, she could barely see the finer points of his bare chest. However, she could make out the width of his shoulders, the definition of his biceps and the light shading at his sternum. She was dying to touch him, investigate the extremely masculine terrain. As if he'd read her mind, he moved forward, leaving little space between them, and flattened her palms against his chest immediately below his collarbone. She took a downward path over his damp skin and when she circled his nipples with her fingertips, she heard the slight catch of his breath. When she slid her hands to his abdomen, she thought he might have stopped breathing. She kept going, using a fingertip to trace the thin trail of hair that disappeared into his waistband.

But that was as far as he allowed her to go. He clasped her wrists, lifted her hands and kissed each palm. Then without fair warning, he pulled her T-shirt up and over her head. She wore only jeans, a pink floral bra and a blanket of goose bumps that had nothing to do with the weather. She predicted he would soon relieve her of the rest of her clothes. Instead, he claimed a boulder to take off his boots and sent her a *What are you waiting for?* look.

"No inhibitions," he said when she failed to remove her bra.

The time had come to kick the self-consciousness to the curb. She sucked in a deep breath, undid the clasp, slipped the straps from her shoulders and added her bra to the clothes heap. "No inhibitions."

The words seemed to shred Zain's control, apparent by the way he pushed off the rock and engaged her in one deep, deadly kiss. After a few moments, he shifted his attention to the column of her throat with light kisses. When his mouth closed over her breast, Madison feathered her hands in his hair in order to stay somewhat steady against the sensual onslaught. So caught up in the pull of his mouth, the feel of his tongue swirling around her nipple, she was only vaguely aware that he'd unfastened her jeans. She became extremely aware when he pushed her pants down her hips, along with her underwear, until both dropped to her ankles.

"No inhibitions," he whispered. "No turning back."

She couldn't turn back if she wanted to, and she didn't. Not in the least. Taking his cue, she used his broad shoulders for support and stepped out of the jeans. Now she was completely naked, while he was still dressed from the waist down. Normally that might make her feel extremely uneasy. Instead, she was incredibly hot, especially when he kissed her again, his hands roving over her bottom, his fingers curling between her thighs.

She wanted him as naked as she was. She wanted him more than she'd wanted anything in quite some time. And it appeared she would get what she wanted when he swept her up into his arms, carried her to the ancient truck and set her on the tailgate. She glanced over her shoulder to discover the bed had been conveniently covered by a colorful quilt, but all her attention soon turned to Zain as he stood in front of her, his hand at his fly.

She was in the buff and barely breathing and drenched. Everywhere. She was also overcome with impatience when Zain failed to remove his slacks.

"Birth control," he grated out as he continued to lower his zipper.

She didn't want to reveal why it wasn't a problem, or burden him with the truth—the chance she could become pregnant was slim to none without medical assistance. This was not the time for sadness or regrets and, most of all, sympathy. "It's not an issue."

"Are you certain?" he asked.

"You're going to have to trust me on this."

That seemed to satisfy his concerns as he took little time shoving his pants down and kicking them away. Now they were both equally undressed and she was extremely impressed. Despite the fact that he'd left on the truck's parking lights, she still wished she could see him better. But even if the sun made an unexpected appearance, Zain wouldn't have given her the chance to assess the details. He hoisted himself onto the tailgate and in a matter of seconds, had her on her back on the makeshift bed.

He hovered above her, his hand resting lightly on her thigh, his gaze leveled on hers. "Do you still trust me?"

Right now, she'd say anything if he'd just get on with it. "Yes."

"Then roll to your side away from me."

Madison wasn't sure where this might be heading, yet she complied because she did trust him. Trusted him not to hurt her. Trusted him to take her on an unforgettable ride.

Zain fitted himself against her back, pushed her

damp hair aside and pressed his lips to her ear. "Clear your mind and think of nothing else but us together." He streamed his hand down her thigh and lifted her leg over his. "Enjoy these moments." He slowly slid his palm down her abdomen. "Pretend this is the only time you will feel this good—" he eased inside her "—again."

The moment Zain hit the mark, Madison shuddered from the sensations. He seemed to time his movement with the stroke of his fingertips, and she responded as if she never had felt this good, because she couldn't recall when she had. He kept a slow, steady pace with both his touch and his body, yet her own body reacted as if they were on a sexual sprint. If she could prolong the involuntary release, she would, but that all-important passion had led to this moment when her body claimed all control. The orgasm arrived quickly in strong spasms, wave after wave of pleasure that seemed to go on forever, though not nearly long enough.

Zain muttered something in Arabic that sound suspiciously like an oath, then pulled out and turned her onto her back. He entered her again, this time not quite as carefully as before, but as promised, he didn't hurt her. He did fuel her fantasies as he rose up on his arms and moved again, harder, faster, his dark gaze firmly fixed on hers. Madison found his powerful thrusts, the continuing rain and the fact they were out in the open highly erotic. And so was the way his jaw went rigid, his eyes closed and his body tensed with the force of his climax that soon came sure and swift.

When Zain collapsed against her, Madison savored the feel of his solid back beneath her palms, even his weight. She didn't exactly appreciate what he had done to her—coaxed her into crossing a line she had never intended to cross. A dangerous boundary that could cost them both if anyone found out.

But even in light of that possibility, she truly believed that this first experience with the king—the *only* experience she could afford—had been absolutely worth the risk.

Unfortunately, it was the last risk she would allow them to take.

Seven

Had it not been for the deluge, Zain would have made love to her again. And again.

Instead, he had carried Madison and set her in the cab. He re-dressed in soaked clothing and gathered hers, only to return to find her wrapped in the dry blanket. Not long after they'd left the lake, she'd settled against his side, her head tipped against his shoulder, and fallen fast asleep. Even when he navigated the rugged terrain, she hadn't woken. But during that time, and since, he had been very aware that she was still naked beneath the blanket. Whenever she stirred, his body did the same. Tonight's brief interlude had not been enough. If he had his way, they would enjoy more of the same, and often, in the upcoming days.

When Madison shifted slightly, Zain glanced at her to see she was still sleeping, looking beautiful and somewhat innocent. She brought out his protective side, though she did not need his protection. She was fiercely independent, fiery and intractable, everything he admired in a woman. Tonight she had proven she possessed an untapped passion that he needed to explore further. She also made him want to right his transgressions and prove to her he owned a measure of honor. He wanted to toss away convention and be with her after the coronation. And that was impossible. Eventually he would be required to marry, and he would not relegate Madison to mistress status. She deserved much better, and so would his future wife. So had his own mother.

That did not preclude him from being with her until the day she left.

When he hit a bump in the road, Madison raised her head and gave him a sleepy smile. "How much longer until we're at the palace?"

"Approximately ten minutes."

She straightened and sent him a panicked look. "You should have woken me earlier," she said as she sorted through the clothes at her side.

"Dressing is not necessary." He preferred she remained naked, as he planned to take her to his bed as soon as they arrived.

"I'm not walking into the royal abode wearing only a blanket." A blanket she tossed aside without regard to her nudity or his discomfort.

He became mesmerized when she lifted her hips and slid her panties into place, followed by her jeans. She picked up her shirt, shook it out, allowing him an extended look at her breasts, the pale pink nipples…

The sound of grating beneath the tires forced his gaze to the road that he'd inadvertently left during his visual exploration. He jerked the truck back onto pavement immediately before he ended up in some unsuspecting citizen's front yard.

"Are you trying to kill us, Zain?"

"I was avoiding a goat."

Madison laughed softly. "An imaginary goat."

He frowned. "It is your fault for distracting me."

"It's your fault for not keeping your eyes on the road."

"I am a man, Madison. You cannot expect me to ignore your state of undress. You should know that after what we shared tonight."

"You're right, and I'm sorry."

He sent another fast glance in her direction to find her completely clothed and smiling. "Are you more comfortable now?"

"I'm very wet."

That prompted a very vivid fantasy, and a return of his erection. "If you will remove your pants again and come over here, I will remedy that."

She shot him a sour look. "You are such a bad boy. No wonder all those women fell all over themselves to be with you."

"Two women."

"Excuse me?"

He finally recognized that she could trust him freely only if he freely gave her accurate information. "I was involved with two women during my time away."

Her blue eyes widened. "You're saying that out of all those highly publicized photos of you escorting various starlets and such, you were only involved with two?"

The disbelief in her voice and expression drove him to disclose the details. "The first woman was older," he continued. "I met Elizabeth through business contacts about a year after I arrived in L.A. My father released only limited funds to me and she assisted with my investments. I owe the majority of my second fortune to her."

"How long were you together?"

Too long for his comfort. "Almost three years."

"What about the second woman?"

This explanation would prove to be more difficult, and much more revealing. Yet for some reason, he wanted Madison to know the facts. Facts few people knew. "Her name was Genevieve. I met her in a café in Paris. I was there for business, she was on sabbatical."

"Then it was only a brief fling?"

"No. I joined her in Africa."

"Africa?" Madison sounded stunned by the revelation. "How long were you there? *Why* were you there?"

"Eighteen months in Ethiopia and, after a three-month break, fifteen months in Nigeria. Genevieve is a humanitarian aid worker. I assisted her with the relief effort by delivering supplies and building temporary shelter."

"Did anyone know your true identity?"

"Only Genevieve." He smiled with remembrance. "She introduced me as Joe Smith."

"That name definitely encourages anonymity," she said. "And to think that all this time, people believed you were holed up with some supermodel, while you were less than a thousand miles away from Bajul being a really stellar guy. Unbelievable."

"Genevieve convinced me I needed to learn the reality of the situation in order to be a better leader." And he had not been prepared for that reality. "I have never seen such desolation. Violence brought about by unrest and ignorance. Famine, starvation and disease brought about by drought and insufficient food and water distribution."

"And that's when you decided to develop your water conservation plans."

He started up the road leading to the castle, relieved that the conversation would soon have to come to an end. "I vowed when my opportunity to rule arrived, I would do everything in my power to prevent the possibility of that devastation in my country. I had not expected the opportunity to arrive so quickly. My plans were to return to Bajul to present my proposals when I received word of my father's death."

"So he never knew about your ideas."

"No." Even if he had, his inflexible father would have rejected them because he had the power to do so. "Regardless, I will never be able to repay Genevieve for forcing me to open my eyes to the possibilities. The experience changed me. She changed me."

"She sounds like a very special woman."

"She was caring and committed and possessed all the attributes I had never acquired." And she'd been much too good for a man whose character had been questionable up to that point in time.

Madison laid a hand on his arm. "But as you've said, you've changed for the better. Not many men in your position would have personally taken on those challenges, and dangerous ones at that. Most would have written a check and returned home."

He appreciated her praise. He greatly appreciated her willingness to listen without judgment. "At times I wish I could have accomplished more, especially when it came to the children."

She sighed. "I know. I remember traveling with my parents to some of the worst poverty-stricken places in the world. The children always suffer the most, even in America."

The memories came back to Zain with the clarity of cut glass. Memories he had never shared with one soul since his return. "I met a special child there. She was around four years of age and an orphan. The workers took charge of her care until a relative could be located. For some reason, she attached herself to me. We spoke different languages, yet we found ways to communicate. Perhaps she appreciated the treats I gave her."

"Or maybe she recognized someone she could trust."

The sincerity in Madison's tone temporarily lifted his spirits. "Her name was Ajo. It means *joyful,* and that suited her. Yet I saw no joy in her when they took her away." He would never forget the way she held out her arms to him, or her tears. The images still haunted him, and at times he felt he had abandoned her.

"Do you know what happened to her?" Madison asked.

He arrived at the gate and raised his hand at the confused guards who, after a slight hesitation, allowed him entry. "Genevieve has been kind enough to keep me apprised of her situation and to deliver the funds I send monthly for Ajo's care. Fortunately, her aunt and uncle see to it she is safe and secure."

"That's wonderful, Zain. But what about your relationship with Genevieve?"

A complex relationship that was never meant to be. "I returned to L.A. when she was reassigned. I had my responsibilities, and she had hers."

"Were you in love with her?"

He was surprised by the query, and uncertain how to answer. He'd cared a great deal for Genevieve, but love had not entered into it. "We both understood from the beginning that our relationship could only be temporary.

We agreed to enjoy each other's company while the opportunity existed."

Madison shifted back to his side and rested her head against his shoulder. "I'm sorry I misjudged you. I bought into the whole 'superficial, arrogant, rich playboy' assumption, just like everyone else did. It's nice to know that couldn't be further from the truth. Despite your issues with your father, it's clear he raised you to be an honorable man."

Anger broke through his remorse. Anger aimed at his patriarch, not at Madison. "My father knew nothing of honor, and he did little to raise me. You may thank Elena for that. I would never take a mistress and force my wife to have a child she did not want. As far as I am concerned, he was responsible for her death due to his careless disregard."

"What happened to her, Zain?"

The strong urge to halt the conversation overcame him. He had already said too much. But Madison's expectant look proved too much, as well. "She was found below the mountain, not far from the lake. Some believe she slipped and fell. Many believe she took her own life due to my father's infidelity. I suppose we will never know the truth."

"I'm so sorry, Zain."

So was he. Sorry that he had almost ruined the evening with regrets. That ended now.

He tipped her face up and kissed her. "We will return to the veranda the same way we left, only we will stay in my room tonight."

She pulled back and slid across the seat away from him. "We're going to walk in the front door, otherwise we'll look guilty. And we're going to stay in separate beds, tonight and every night until I leave."

That would not suffice. "I would prefer you sleep in my bed the majority of the night after we make love. As long as we've parted by morning, no one will be the wiser."

She folded the jacket's hem back and forth. "We can't take the risk that someone will find out. I had a wonderful time tonight, but we can't be together in that way again."

How many times in his youth had he said something of a similar nature to a woman? "That is unacceptable. How to you expect me to pretend I do not want you when I do?" More than she knew. More than he realized until he faced the prospect of not having her.

"We're going to limit our alone time together."

"You've said that before."

"This time I mean it, Zain. I am not going to be responsible for a scandal that could ruin all the work we're doing to restore your image."

Zain gripped the wheel and stared straight ahead. "Then you lied when you said you trust me."

"I do trust you, and so should your people. I admire and respect you even more now. But when I said I didn't trust myself, I wasn't talking about sex. I've already blurred the personal and professional lines and I can't afford to become more emotionally involved with you than I already am. Now we need to go inside before they come looking for us."

Before Zain could respond, she was out the door and walking toward the path leading to the front entrance. He left the truck and caught up with her in the courtyard flanking the front steps. After clasping her arm, he turned her to face him. "I will honor your wishes. I will allow you your blessed distance, but not before I give you this."

He crushed her against him and kissed her with all the desperation he experienced at the moment. He expected her to fight him, and when instead she responded, he realized she wanted him as much as he wanted her. As much as he needed her for reasons that defied logic. He agreed with her on one point—this was not only about sex.

Then she wrested from his grasp, looking as if he'd struck her. "Don't make this more complicated than it already is, Zain."

Madison hurried around the corner and by the time he reached the stone steps, she had already disappeared through the doors.

Once inside, he was met by a security contingent and Deeb. "You are all dismissed," he said in Arabic. "No harm has come to me to warrant this attention." Not the kind of harm they would assume.

He ascended the stairs only to have Deeb stop him on the second-floor landing. "Your brother asked me to summon you to his study upon your return."

Confronting Rafiq was the last thing he needed. "I have no desire to speak to him."

"What shall I tell him, Emir?"

Tell him to go to hell. "I will see him in the morning."

Zain arrived at the corridor leading to his quarters in time to see the door to Madison's room close, shutting him out.

Perhaps she could easily dismiss him and what they had shared tonight, but he would wager she would suffer for the decision to avoid him. So would he.

But he would do as he had promised and hoped she decided they should take advantage of what little time together they had left. In the meantime, he would prepare to spend the first of several long, sleepless nights.

* * *

Ten days had passed since Madison had enjoyed a decent night's sleep, and she had Zain to thank for that. Not only had he upheld his promise to give her space, he'd downright ignored her. He'd avoided all eye contact when they'd been together, and he'd only spoken to her when she had spoken first. The two times they'd briefly found themselves alone following one of his myriad meetings, not once had he mentioned their night together, nor had he delivered even the slightest innuendo. He hadn't joined her and Rafiq for dinner, but at least she'd had a chance to get to know the older brother, who was highly intelligent and not quite as serious as she'd once assumed.

She truly didn't know if Zain was simply pouting, or proving a point. Either way, she admittedly missed their intimate conversations. Missed kissing him, as well. She definitely missed her former common sense, which had apparently followed the rain out of town.

Zain had been right to remain in strictly business mode, and business was exactly what she needed to focus on today, and each day until the coronation.

Madison sought out Elena and found her in the kitchen, where the wonderful scents permeating the area caused her stomach to rumble even though she'd had enough breakfast to kill an elephant. Evidently she'd been making up for the lack of sex by eating her way through the kingdom.

"That smells marvelous," she said as she approached the metal prep table holding a platter full of puffed pastries.

Elena smiled and gestured toward the fare. "Please try one. The chef prepared the samples for Prince Zain's approval, but he refused. He said he did not care if they served water and wheat at the wedding reception."

Clearly His Royal Pain in the Arse had forgotten they'd added guests to the list, who could be beneficial to his reign. But hey, if he didn't want to try the goodies, she certainly would. "Thanks, I believe I will take a bite or two." Or three, she decided when the flaky crust and creamy filling practically melted in her mouth.

After Madison had consumed five of the canapés, she looked up to meet Elena's quizzical look. "Tell the chef he's hit a home run with this." As if the guy would understand a baseball analogy. "Better still, tell him they're perfect."

"I will pass that on," Elena said. "I will also tell him to prepare double for you."

Great. She'd demonstrated she had serious etiquette issues. "That's not necessary. I eat when I'm nervous, and this whole reception has me on edge. I hope we're doing the right thing by not having a separate gathering prior to the coronation."

"Have you consulted the new king about forgoing that honor?"

"Actually, it was his idea. He's not being all that cooperative these days. Maybe he's a bit anxious about officially becoming His Majesty in less than two weeks."

"Or perhaps he is being denied something he wants more than the crown."

Madison faked ignorance. "A new sports car?"

Elena raised a thin brow. "You may fool the rest of the household, *cara,* but you are not fooling me. I know you and Prince Zain stole away without notifying anyone of your departure, and returned in wet clothing."

The palace apparently had spies in place and gossip down to a science. "He wanted to show me the lake and we got caught in a storm." A firestorm. "That's all there was to it."

"Are you certain of that?"

She knew better than to try to lie to a wise bird like Elena. She also knew not to reveal too much, even if she thought she could trust her with the truth. "Wise or not, we have developed a friendship. He's even begun to confide in me about his past and, most important, his goals. That's been beneficial for me, since I've been preparing the speech he'll deliver next week." A speech he would probably reject.

She couldn't miss the concern on Elena's face. "What has he said about the king and queen?"

"Since he took me into his confidence, I don't feel I should say more." She'd already come down with foot-in-mouth disease to go with the voracious appetite.

"Anything you could say to me, *cara mia,* I have already heard in the many years I've been here. The staff talks about things they know nothing about, and most is not true."

She did have a point. "He mentioned something about the king having mistresses, and that he believes that was directly related to the queen's death."

Elena grabbed the platter and took it to the counter next to the massive industrial sink. "Go on," she said, keeping her back to Madison.

The fact Elena didn't deny the conjecture was very telling. "He also said that the queen was forced to have a third child against her will."

Elena spun around, a touch of anger calling out from her amber eyes. "That is not true. The queen would have done anything to have another child. And furthermore, the king was the one who only wanted two children, yet he was so devoted to her, he gave her what she desired. Sadly, Adan did not aid in her happiness."

"Was she so unhappy that she took her own life?"

"I would not begin to speculate on that, and neither should you."

Madison held up her hands. "I'm sorry I've upset you. I was only repeating what Zain told me." Darn if she hadn't done it again—called him by his given name.

Elena sighed. "It is not your fault, *cara*. And I beg of you to please not repeat what I have said."

She found it odd that Elena would want to conceal the information from the boys she had practically raised. "Don't you think the princes have a right to know the truth?"

"Some secrets are best left in the past." Elena picked up a towel and began to twist it, a sure sign of distress. "Did you require anything else from me? If not, I have some work to attend to."

Madison knew not to press the matter any further. She needed Elena as an ally, not an enemy. "Actually, I was wondering if you had a final guest list for the reception. I want to go over it with His Highness." Provided he didn't toss her out on her posterior, injuring her pride.

"Yes, I do." Elena walked into the office, emerged a few moments later and handed her two pages full of names. "You'll see that I have made a separate column for the prospective queen candidates and their fathers. I thought you would find that helpful."

She found it appalling. "I suppose Prince Zain will appreciate that information. He can come prepared for when they converge upon him."

Elena surprisingly patted Madison's cheek. "Do not worry, *cara*. He will find none of them to his liking as long as you are here." With that, the woman smiled, returned to the office and closed the door.

Obviously no one could pull the wool over Elena's eyes, and that could present some complications if Madison didn't remain strong in Zain's presence.

Not a problem. The way things were going, she'd be lucky if he ever seriously spoke to her again, let alone touched her.

Eight

He wanted nothing more than to touch her. Only a slight touch. Or perhaps not so slight at that.

Since Madison's arrival in the study, Zain had engaged in several fantasies that involved taking her down on the sofa where she sat reciting names that mattered not to him.

"Who is Layali Querishi?" she asked. "That sounds familiar."

He fixated on Madison's blue blouse, which could easily be unbuttoned, allowing access to her breasts. "She is a sultan's daughter and a popular singer."

"And gorgeous." She crossed her legs, causing the skirt's hem to ride higher on her thighs. "I remember seeing an article about her Australian tour."

"I do not recall her looks." Nor did he care about them. He only cared about running his hands up Madison's skirt as a reminder of what they had given up for the sake of professionalism.

"Do you think that's a good idea?"

Madison's question startled Zain into believing he might have voiced his thoughts. "What are you referring to?"

"Pay attention, Your Highness."

He had been paying attention—to her. "My apologies. I have a lot weighing on my mind." And a heavy weight behind his fly.

"I said do you think it's a good idea to seat all these women together at the same table? That's grounds for a queen candidate catfight."

He could not hold back his smile. "Some might find that thoroughly entertaining."

"Or thoroughly in bad taste. I suggest we separate them to avoid bloodshed."

He started to suggest they discard the list and move on to something much more pleasurable, when a series of raps sounded at the door. Familiar raps that readily identified the offending party.

Madison consulted her watch. "It's late. I can't imagine who would be stopping in this time of night, unless it's Mr. Deeb."

"It's not Deeb."

"Then who is it?"

"My brother."

Thankful his coat sufficiently hid his current state, Zain rounded the desk and opened the door to Adan wearing his standard military-issue flight suit and a cynical smile. He made a circular sweeping gesture with his arm and bowed dramatically. "Greetings, His Majesty, king of the surfing sheikhs."

He had not mentioned that pastime to Madison, but she definitely knew now. He wanted to send Adan on his way but instead gave him the required manly embrace. "When did you arrive?"

"I flew in a while ago." Adan leaned around him. "And who is this lovely lady?"

"I'm Madison Foster." Zain turned to see her standing in front of the sofa. "And you must be Prince Adan."

"The one and the only." Adan crossed the room, took Madison's hand and kissed it. "Are you one of my brother's California conquests?"

"She is a political consultant," Zain added in an irritable tone. "Which means she is off-limits to you."

Adan released her hand but offered up a devil-may-care grin. "I have only honorable intentions."

She returned his smile as she reclaimed her seat. "You also have a very British accent."

"He has an aversion to authority," Zain said. "He spent most of his formative years in a military boarding school in the U.K."

Adan attempted to look contrite. "I have since learned to respect authority and take orders, as long as they are not delivered by my brothers."

Zain wanted to order him out of the room. "Considering the lateness of the hour, I am certain you are ready to retire."

"Actually, I am wide-awake." He had the audacity to drop down beside Madison and drape his arm over the back of the sofa. "How long will you be here?"

"Ms. Foster will be with *me* until after the coronation," Zain answered before she could respond. "And we still have much to accomplish tonight."

"We can take up where we left off tomorrow," Madison said as she came to her feet. "I'm sure you two have a lot of catching up to do after all these years."

Adan clasped her wrist and pulled her back down

beside him, sparking Zain's barely contained fury. "I visited Zain in Los Angeles less than six months ago. In fact, I was his guest at least once a year during his time there."

Many times an unwelcome guest, as he was now. "For that reason, he should return to his quarters so that we might resume our tasks."

Adan ignored him and took the pages from Madison. "What is this?"

"We're going over the guest list for the upcoming wedding reception," she said.

He leaned closer to her. "Am I on it?"

She seemed unaffected by his nearness, and that only served to anger Zain more. "Since you're in the wedding party, there's no need to add your name."

Adan perused the pages for a few moments. "Ah, I see we have a bevy of prospective brides in attendance. Najya Toma's much too young. Taalah Wasem is too stuffy. And I had hoped to claim the third one as my own. No one would turn down a chance to bed Layali Querishi." He winked. "Of course, she is not quite as beautiful as you."

Zain had had quite enough. "If you are finished with your attempts to seduce my employee, I suggest you retire to your quarters now so that we may resume our duties."

Adan reluctantly came to his feet. "You are beginning to sound like Rafiq. Did you leave your sense of humor in the States?"

"Did you leave your sense of decorum in your jet?"

"Women are quite taken with my jet."

Zain pointed at the door. "Out. Now."

Adan had the audacity to laugh. "I can take a hint, brother. And I certainly understand why you would want

Ms. Foster all to yourself." He regarded Madison again. "It has been a pleasure, madam. Should you need protection from this rogue, feel free to notify me immediately."

She needed protection from his rogue brother. "I assure you, Adan, Ms. Foster is in good hands and does not require your assistance."

Adan sent Madison another smile. "Then I will bid you both good-night."

After Adan thankfully left, Zain closed the door and tripped the lock. He turned back to Madison and launched into a tirade on the heels of his anger. "Although you obviously enjoyed my brother's attention, you should know that he is a master of seduction. Stay clear of him."

"That's rich, coming from you." She tossed the papers aside and sighed. "Not to mention he's practically a baby, and he seems perfectly harmless."

He took a few steps toward her. "He is five years my junior. That makes him twenty-eight, and a man."

"And he's three years younger than me, so in my eyes, that makes him cougar bait."

He had not realized she was over thirty, but then he had never asked her age. "Adan would not care if you were twice his age. He recognizes a beautiful woman, he is anything but harmless and he has designs on you."

She rolled her eyes. "Stop playing the jealous monarch, Zain."

He was not playing. "I am only concerned about your well-being."

She tossed the pages aside. "Really? For the past few days, you haven't seemed at all concerned about my well-being, or anything else, for that matter. You've barely given me the time of day."

And it had nearly destroyed him. "I am giving you space as you've requested."

"You're giving me the cold shoulder, and I don't deserve that."

"And you believe I deserve this torture?"

"What torture?"

He slid his hands in his pockets and took two more slow steps. "Each time you are near me, I can only think about touching you. Ignoring you is my only means of self-defense."

"You could at least be civil."

When he reached her, he took off his jacket and draped it over the back of the sofa. "Civility is the last thing on my mind when you're dressed as you are now."

She looked down before returning her gaze to his. "It's a plain blouse and knee-length skirt, Zain, and I've been dressing this way since we met. It's more than decent."

Decent yes, but his thoughts were not. "And I have suffered because of your choices."

She rested her elbow on the back of the sofa and rubbed her forehead. "Fine. I'll wear a full-body burlap sack from now on."

"It would not matter what you are wearing. I would still imagine you naked."

"And that makes you just like every other man who comes in contact with a female."

He leaned forward and braced his palms on the cushions on either side of her hips. "Is that what I am to you, Madison? Only one more man who wants you? Was our lovemaking nothing more than a diversion?"

Unmistakable desire flashed in her eyes. "It was… It was…"

"Remarkable?"

"Unwise."

He brushed a kiss across her cheek before nuzzling her neck. "Tell me you do not want to experience it again, and I will leave you alone."

"You're asking me to lie."

He touched his lips to hers. "I am asking you to admit that you still want me. I want to hear you say that you are as consumed by thoughts of us as I am."

"Stop making it so hard to resist you, Zain."

Using the sofa's back for support, he lifted her hand and pressed it against his fly. "You are making it hard on me, Madison."

She rubbed her thumb along the ridge. "That sounds like a very personal problem to me."

He kissed her then, a kiss hot enough to ignite the room. But when she tried to pull him down beside her, he resisted and straightened.

She glared up at him. "I get it now. You're teasing me and then you're going to walk out of here just to punish me."

"I promise I have no intention of punishing you." He lowered to the floor on his knees to fulfill his greatest fantasy. "Unless you consider absolute pleasure a form of punishment."

When he reached beneath her skirt and slid her panties down, she released a slight gasp. And when he parted her legs, she trembled. He kept his gaze leveled on hers as he kissed the inside of one thigh, then the other, and prepared for a protest. Instead, she remained silent as her chest rapidly rose and fell in anticipation.

"Unbutton your blouse and lower your bra," he said, though he realized she might not answer his demand if she believed he had gone too far.

Yet she surprised him by releasing the buttons with

shaking fingers before reaching beneath the back of the blouse to unclasp the bra.

Seeing her eyes alight with excitement and her breasts exposed was almost his undoing. As badly as he wanted to dispense with formality and seat himself deep inside her, he had something else in mind. Yet before he sought his ultimate destination, he had one final question. "Tell me you want me to keep going."

She exhaled slowly. "You know I do, dammit."

The first curse she'd ever uttered in his presence served to excite him even more. "Then say it."

"I want you to do it."

That was all he needed to hear. He pushed her skirt up to her waist for better access, slipped his hands beneath her hips and lowered his mouth between her trembling legs. He watched her face to gauge her reaction as he teased her with the tip of his tongue, varying the pressure to prolong the pleasure.

When her eyes momentarily drifted shut, he stopped and lifted his head. "Look at me, Madison. I want you to see what I am doing to you."

She blinked twice as if in a trance. "I don't think I can."

"Yes, you can, and you will."

When their gazes locked, he went back to his exploration, more thoroughly this time. She gripped the cushions and lifted her hips to meet his mouth, indicating she was close to reaching a climax. And as she tipped her head back and released a low moan, Zain refused to let up until her frame and expression went slack.

After her breathing slowed and her eyes closed again, he rose to his feet. Leaving her now would be difficult, but he felt he had no choice. He turned and started toward the door, only to halt midstride when she asked, "Where are you going?"

He faced her to find she was clutching her blouse closed, a mixture of ire and confusion in her expression. "I am going to bed, and you should, as well. You should be relaxed enough to enjoy a restful sleep." He regrettably would not. He would lie awake for hours, aching for her and wondering when he would have her again. If he would ever have her again.

"Oh, no, you don't," she said. "You're not going to just leave me here alone after you've somehow managed to turn me into some sort of wild animal in heat."

"I know you, Madison, and this wildness is the part of you that you've kept concealed from the world, and from yourself. You have simply never met a man who encourages that side of you before now. I am that man."

She released the blouse, allowing it to gape open. "A real man would come over and finish what he started."

It took all his resolve not to answer her challenge. "From this point forward, you will have to come to me. But mark my words, we will finish this."

Mark my words, we will finish this...

To this point, Madison hadn't given Zain that satisfaction, although he'd given her plenty during their little office interlude. She'd managed to afford the same courtesy he had shown her by turning the tables on him. She'd made a point to avoid him the past three days, but unfortunately, she couldn't avoid him tonight.

While she claimed a corner of the banquet hall, nursing a mineral water and a solid case of jealousy, the imminent king stood at the front of the room, basking in female attention. Who could blame them? He was a tall, dark presence dressed in a black silk suit, light gray shirt and a perfect-match tie. Both his looks and his status had earned him more than his share of attention. She'd basically been relegated to wallflower status, after she'd made the required rounds among the dignitaries and diplomats she'd personally invited. Normally she didn't like being invisible, yet tonight she didn't care if she blended into the background. It didn't matter one whit if no one noticed her.

"You are looking exceedingly lovely tonight, Ms. Foster."

Madison glanced to her left and met the dimpled baby Mehdi's charming smile. She still couldn't get over his lack of resemblance to his older brothers, who could almost pass as twins. Where their eyes were almost black, Adan's were golden and his hair was much lighter. That didn't make him any less gorgeous in a boyish sort of way. "Thank you, Your Highness."

"Tonight you should refer to me as Adan." He took a step back and studied the crimson cocktail dress she'd chosen instead of the black one Zain had requested she wear all those weeks ago. "Red certainly becomes you."

She smoothed a hand over the skirt. "I worried it might be overkill."

"Your beauty has almost killed some of our elder statesmen. You'll know who they are as they are holding their ribs where their wives have landed elbows throughout the evening."

She couldn't hold back a laugh over that image. "Don't be ridiculous."

"I am only being observant." He nodded toward Zain. "My brother the king has certainly noticed. He has watched your every move all night, and he's presently staring at us, the fires of hell in his eyes."

Madison turned her attention to Zain and confirmed

he had one heck of a glare leveled on them. "He's too involved with his admirers to care about me."

"He cannot give them his proper attention when you are all that he sees."

"That's ridiculous."

"That is the truth." He leaned close to her ear. "Right now he believes I am propositioning you, and if he knew that for certain, he would come over here and wrap his hands around my throat."

She couldn't believe he would even think that about Zain, let alone voice it. "He wouldn't do that. He's your brother."

Adan straightened and smiled. "He is a man obsessed with a woman. I have no idea what you have done to bewitch him, but your spell has effectively created a monster. I have never known Zain to be so possessive. Perhaps he is caught in a web of love and he has no idea how to free himself."

A web of lust, maybe, but Madison didn't buy the love theory. Anxious to end the troubling conversation, she opted for a topic change. "The wedding was nice, although I didn't understand one word of the vows." She also didn't understand how a bride could have looked so sad on her wedding day.

"You did not miss much," Adan said. "It was a merger. The culmination of a business arrangement born out of obligation. An obligation I will eventually face. But since I have no direct claim to the throne, I intend to enjoy my freedom until I am at least forty. Regrettably, Zain is not as fortunate. He will be expected to marry a suitable bride as soon as possible."

Madison didn't need to be reminded of that, nor did she need to encourage more discussion about Zain by commenting on the antiquated tradition. "Speaking of the bride and groom, I haven't seen them in a while."

"They have retired to the marriage bed," Adan said as he snatched a glass of fruity punch from the roving waiter's tray. "And by now Rafiq has confirmed that his bride is not a virgin. Of course, he will not care as long as she spreads her legs in an effort to produce the mandatory heir."

She frowned. "That's rather crass, and how do you know for sure she isn't a virgin?"

"Because another Mehdi brother had her first."

Surely not… "Zain?"

Adan downed the rest of his drink and set the glass on the nearby side table. "Yours truly."

Madison did well to hide her shock. "You slept with your brother's wife?"

"Future wife," he said. "And I did not instigate it. I had recently arrived home from the academy to celebrate my seventeenth birthday at a friend's house. Rima came by after having argued with her true love. She was looking for consolation wherever she could find it. I happened to be searching for a willing woman to give me my first experience. I tried to refuse but, alas, I succumbed to her charms. It was, as they say, the perfect storm."

A perfect mess, in Madison's opinion. "And Rafiq never wondered where she'd gone after they argued?"

He sent her a practiced smirk. "I said she argued with her true love. I did not say she argued with Rafiq."

She had somehow become embroiled in a real-live Arabian soap opera. "Then who is it?" Reconsidering the question, she raised her hands, palms forward. "Never mind. I don't want to know."

When Madison noticed one young woman standing on tiptoe and whispering in Zain's ear, she'd seen enough.

Her feet hurt and her heart ached. She only wanted to crawl into bed and throw the covers over her head. That probably wouldn't stop the images of the king taking another willing woman into his bed.

She set her glass next to Adan's and smiled. "Since the crowd seems to be dwindling, I'm going to head to my quarters now. It's been nice talking to you." And very, very interesting.

He lifted her hand for a kiss. "Should you require a man's undivided attention, I am on the second floor in the room at the end of the hall."

She tugged her hand away and patted his cheek. "You, Adan, are too charming for your own good, and I'm really much too old for you."

"As was Rima."

She wasn't going to jump into that sorry situation again. "Good night."

Without waiting for Adan's reply, she hurried through the expansive ballroom and bore down on the double doors that led into one of the many courtyards. Since the building was separate from the palace proper, she found the surroundings seriously confusing, particularly when only dimly lit by random lights alongside the various pathways. Deeb had accompanied her to the reception, but he had long since left, and now she was on her own. That shouldn't present a major problem. She had a master's in political science, a good sense of direction and she'd always excelled at geography. Give her a map and she could find her way anywhere. Too bad she didn't have a map of the jumbled of walkways.

Madison chose the most direct path and immediately arrived at an intersection. She couldn't remember whether to go right or left and wished she'd paid more attention on her way there. She could see the looming palace, but had no clue how to get there. Maybe she should flip a coin—heads, right; tails, left. Maybe she would end up in Yemen if she took a wrong turn.

Luckily she heard approaching footsteps behind her and pivoted around, expecting to see a security guard who could show her the way. She wasn't prepared to see Zain walking toward her instead.

She refused to do this, her prime motivation for taking off down the hedge-lined brick path to her immediate right. At the moment, she didn't care if she wound up seeking shelter in a caretaker's cottage, as long as she could escape before she did something totally foolish, like taking the pretty prince down into the hedges and having her wicked way with him.

"Madison, wait."

She didn't dare look back. "No."

"You cannot continue."

"Yes, I can. Watch me."

"You are about to hit a dead end."

No sooner than he'd said it, Madison did it—almost ran smack dab into a brick tower with a nice little water feature set off to the side of a small bench.

She had no choice but to face the music, or in this case, the monarch. "Go back to your guests, Zain," she said when she turned around.

He loosened his tie and collar. "The guests have all departed."

She folded her arms beneath her breasts. "You couldn't entice even one of those nubile young creatures into your bedroom?"

He slipped the single button on his coat. "They did not hold my interest."

If he made one move to undress, she would have to resort to hedge-diving. "I'm sorry to hear that. Now if you would kindly point me in the right direction, I'll be on my way."

When he stalked forward, she retreated, once again finding herself backed against a wall. "I am not letting you leave until you understand that being without you is killing me," he said.

"You seemed quite alive to me tonight."

"Those women meant nothing to me." He braced one hand above her head and used the other to slip the wide strap down her shoulder. "Seeing you in this dress made matters worse, as did watching you with Adan. Had he touched you again, I would have crossed the room and wrapped my hands around his neck."

She almost laughed when she recalled Adan had said those exact words. "You can't go around beating up any boy who pays attention to me while I'm here. And I won't be here much longer."

"Precisely," he said before he leaned down and kissed her bare shoulder. "Our time together is limited and I do not wish to waste more than we already have."

"What happened to me coming to you?" Better still, what was happening to her determination to resist him?

"My patience is in tatters. We have been playing the avoidance game long enough. It's time to release our pride and admit that we need to be together. I *need* to be with you."

And heaven help her, she needed to be with him as much as she needed air, which seemed to leave her when he streamed his hand over the curve of her hip.

If he wanted to finish this once and for all, then they would finish it, even if it meant going out in a blaze of glory. "If you need me that much, stop talking and kiss me."

He did, with enough power to light up the country.

Before Madison knew it, Zain had her bodice pulled down, his mouth on her breast and his hand between her legs. Somewhere in the back of her mind, she realized she should tell him to stop and take it to the bedroom before they went any further. But she was too weak with wanting and too far gone to halt the madness.

And madness it was when he pushed her panties down and did the same with his slacks before he wrapped her legs around his hips and drove into her. His intense thrusts blew her mind and propelled her to the edge of orgasmic bliss. That one-time foreign sound began to form in her throat, only to be halted when Zain planted his palm over her mouth.

At that point, she heard the nearby voices, saw movement between the break of the trees. Knowing that could get caught only heightened the dangerous pleasure, and brought about a climax that shook her to the core. She could tell Zain had been affected, too, by the way he tensed and released a guttural groan in her ear, followed by that same single harsh Arabic word.

The sound of their ragged breathing seemed to echo throughout the area, and Madison hoped the passing party had moved out of earshot. Zain loosened his hold, allowing her legs to slide down where she fortunately found her footing. She still felt as if she were on shaky emotional ground.

For that reason, she had to get away from him. "We need to return to our respective rooms before Deeb sends out a posse and they catch you with your pants down."

He planted both palms on the wall and rested his forehead against hers, his eyes tightly closed. "When I think about you leaving me, even only for a moment, it sickens me."

She could relate to that. "We knew my leaving was

inevitable, Zain. The more time we spend together, the harder it will be to say goodbye." At least for her.

He raised his head, some unidentifiable emotion in his eyes. "Stay with me tonight, Madison. All night. I want to wake in the morning to find you beside me."

And that seemed like a recipe for disaster when it came to her heart. "But—"

His soft kiss quelled her protest. "I am begging you to stay."

Madison had stayed with Zain that night, and every night for the past week. They had grown so close, and she had become so lost in him, she'd begun to believe she didn't know where he ended and she began. And that frightened her, but not enough to stop sleeping in his bed, and waking up every morning to his wonderful face. This morning was no exception.

When a ribbon of light streamed through a break in the heavy curtains covering the window, Madison rolled to her side, bent her elbow and supported her cheek with her palm. She took a few moments to capture a good, long look at the beautiful sleeping prince. The prince who would become king in two days.

His dark lashes fanned out beneath his closed eyes and his gorgeous mouth twitched slightly, as if he might smile. The navy satin sheet rode low on his hips, exposing the crease of his pelvic bone and the stream of hair below his navel. Her face heated when she remembered following that path last night with her lips, causing Zain to squirm when she kept right on going.

She realized she was only a shell of her former self—the woman who had repressed her sexual nature for fear of losing control. Lately, losing control had been preferable when it came to making love with Zain, in many ways, and in many different places—in the study at noon, in the shower several times, in the tunnel leading to the lower-level grounds and on the veranda after midnight, even knowing extra guards had been posted at the corners of the building on all levels. Yet some of the most memorable times came when they took walks in the garden, holding hands and stealing innocent kisses. And the long talks had meant the world to her, conversations about politics and policy and sometimes their pasts. Zain had even reluctantly admitted he harbored some guilt over not having the opportunity to say goodbye to his father, and that made her ache for him.

But the one defining moment in their relationship happened two mornings ago, when she'd awakened alone in his bed, with an orchid on her pillow and a note that read, "You make my days, and my nights, worthwhile."

She'd realized she loved him then. Loved him more than she ever thought possible. Yet none of that mattered. In forty-eight brief hours, he would enter a new era as the king, signaling the end of theirs.

But she still had today—an important day for Zain— so she shook off the downhearted thoughts and kissed his bare shoulder. When he didn't respond, she pressed another kiss on his unshaven jaw, then propped her chin on his chest. "Time to get up, Your Sexiness."

His eyes drifted open and his lips curled into a smile. She would store that smile in the memory bank to get her through the lonely days to come. "I am up," he said in his sexy morning voice.

Madison caught his drift and lifted the sheet. Yes, he had definitely arisen to the occasion, as usual. "I'll rephrase that," she said as she dropped the covers back into place. "You need to get out of bed, get dressed and get ready to address your subjects. On that note, I don't know why you won't give my speech suggestions even a little bit of considera—"

He rudely interrupted her light lecture when he flipped her onto her back and rubbed against her. As far as bedside manners went, she couldn't complain. "My royal staff yearns for your attention," he said as he buried his face in her neck.

She had to laugh over that one. "Aren't we just the king of bad euphemisms this morning?"

He lifted his head and grinned. "I have more descriptive ones, if you'd like to hear them."

Before she could object, he had his lips to her ear and her body reeling with possibilities when he recited a litany of crude, albeit sexy, suggestions. When he looked at her again, she faked shock. "Oh, my. Did you minor in dirty words in college, or have you been watching too much cable TV?"

His cupped her breast in his palm. "You bring out the savage in me."

She could say the same for him. He made her want to growl, especially at the moment when he set his hands in motion all over her bare body.

Right when he had her where he wanted her—hot, and bothered and almost begging—the bedside phone began to ring. He eased inside her at the same moment he picked up the receiver. Madison marveled over his ability to multitask, then became mortified when she recognized Rafiq's voice on the other end of the line.

"I am currently occupied," Zain said. "However, when I am able to pull myself away from this most pressing matter, I will be downstairs in the study."

After he hung up, Madison laughed. "You are so bad."

He frowned. "Last night you told me I was very good."

"No. That's what you told me."

The teasing quickly ended as they concentrated on their lovemaking, on each other with a familiarity normally reserved for longtime lovers. But they were so attuned to one another now, it seemed as if they had been lovers forever. And in the aftermath, when Zain's gentle, whispered words of praise floated into Madison's ears, she started to cry. For some reason, she'd done a lot of that lately, but never in front of him.

As he folded her into his arms and stroked her hair, he didn't question her about the tears. He only held her close to his heart until they finally subsided.

"I'm sorry," she said after she recovered from the meltdown. "I guess my leaving is starting to sink in."

"I am trying not to think about it," he said. "Otherwise, I might not get through my duties today."

She wanted so badly to tell him she loved him, but what would be the point? Nothing had changed. Nothing would. She was still the unsuitable American, and he was still the Arabian king steeped in tradition, destined to choose one of his kind.

So she raised her head and gave him her sunniest smile, even though she wanted to sob. "Speaking of your duties, the time has come for you to impress the masses, the way you've continually impressed me."

His dark eyes were so intense, it stole her breath. "Madison, I..." His gaze drifted away with his words.

"You what?"

When he finally looked at her again, he seemed almost detached. "I want to thank you for all that you've done. I would not have gotten through this process had it not been for your support."

That comment was as dry as the desert, and not at all what she wanted to hear. "And to think you almost sent me packing that first night."

"I am glad you fought me on that, and I will never forget our time together."

Funny, that sounded a lot like an early goodbye. Maybe he was just doing some advance preparation, and she should take his cue. "You're welcome, Your Highness. Now that the party's over, it's time to take care of business."

Nine

He had arrived at this first of two monumental moments with a certain confidence, and he had not managed that alone. Unbeknownst to Madison, he had every intention of taking her advice and speaking from the heart. If only he had been able to do that this morning. The one word he had not been able to say—had never said to any woman—had stalled on his lips. Committing to that emotion would only complicate matters more. She was bound to leave, and he was bound to duty as the leader of his country.

"They're ready for you, Emir," Deeb said as he opened the doors to the veranda.

"Good luck, Your Highness," Madison said from behind him.

Since their last conversation that morning, a certain formality had formed between them. Yet he could not consider that now, nor did he dare look at her and meet the sadness in her eyes. "Thank you," he said as he left her to deliver the most important speech of his life.

He moved onto the balcony containing enough guards to populate a military installation. After taking a few moments to gather his thoughts, he stepped behind the podium, and the cameras began to flash. Zain surveyed the masses spread out on the grounds as far as the eye could see. Among those in the immediate vicinity, he spotted a few familiar faces—Maysa, Malik and his family, as well as several childhood friends—and that served to further bolster his self-assurance. Many of the others looked both eager and somewhat suspicious, most likely because they were waiting for him to fail. He refused to fail.

He pulled the pages containing the prepared speech, then on afterthought, set them aside. He also ignored the teleprompter that Madison insisted he have so he wouldn't falter. If his words did not come out perfectly, so be it. His country would then know he was not perfect, and that suited him fine. He had his flaws, but he had the best of intentions. Now he had to convince the country of that.

After adjusting the microphone, Zain began to speak, immediately silencing the restless crowd. He began with outlining his water conservation plan, which garnered minor applause. He continued by insisting that education was the key to prosperity, and he vowed to fund school improvements. He went on to talk about the importance of family, his love for their country and his commitment to its people. He spoke about his father in respectful terms, highlighting all that the former king had accomplished during his forty-year reign, and that he would proudly serve by his example. That earned him a roar from the crowd and shouts of approval. Perhaps he had finally arrived.

Yet as he remained to acknowledge their support, he could not help but wish Madison was at his side. Wish that he had the means to change tradition and choose his bride by virtue of her attributes, not her dowry. But that would present the possibility of rejection not only by the council, but also the traditionalists who expected him to marry one of their own. And even if he could successfully lobby for that change, would he subject Madison to this life? Would he risk destroying her sense of independence in exchange for assuming the role of his queen? A role that had left some women emotionally broken, including his own mother. He then recalled when Madison had said she would never give up her life for any man, and he could not in good conscience ask that of her, even if the thought of letting her go sickened him.

When he felt the tap on his shoulder, he turned to find Deeb, not Madison, as he had hoped. "The press is waiting in the conference room, Emir."

One hurdle jumped, yet another awaited him—answering intrusive questions. "I will be along shortly." First, he planned to seek Madison's approval, a move he would have never made before her, and not because he lacked respect for women. Because he had been that inflexible. She had changed him more than he realized. More than any woman had, even Genevieve. Madison had served as his touchstone for the past month and, in many ways, had given him the strength to survive the chaos. Her opinion mattered to him. She mattered to him, much more than she should.

With a final wave, Zain returned to the study to find Madison seated across the room in front of the corner television, watching the international analysis of his address. He approached the chair and laid a hand on her shoulder to garner her attention. "Did Deeb interpret for you?"

When her frame went rigid, he removed his hand. "Yes, Deeb translated, and you did a remarkable job. For the most part."

When he moved between her and the TV to ask what she hadn't liked, he noticed she did not look well. Her skin was pale and a light sheen of perspiration covered her forehead. "Are you feeling all right?"

"I'm fine," she said as she abruptly stood. "It's a little warm in here."

When she swayed, he clasped her arm to steady her. "You should sit down again."

She tugged out of his grasp. "I said I am perfectly fine, Your Highness. I'm just going to…"

Her eyes suddenly closed, her lips parted slightly, and as she began to fall, Zain caught her in his arms and carried her to the sofa. He had never felt such concern, such fear and such anger over his staff's failure to immediately act.

He turned his ire on Deeb. "Do not stand there like an imbecile. Summon Dr. Barad. Now!"

Madison came awake slowly, feeling somewhat confused and disoriented. She had no idea how she'd ended up on Zain's office couch, although she did recall being dizzy and starting to free-fall. After that, nothing but a big, black void.

When she raised her head from the sofa's arm, an unfamiliar female voice said, "Stay still for a few more moments, Ms. Foster."

The owner of that voice finally came into focus—an exotic woman with dark almond-shaped eyes and long brown hair pulled back into a braid. "Who are you?" Madison asked in a sandpaper voice.

"Maysa Barad." She lifted a stethoscope from a black bag set on the coffee table. "I'm a local physician and friend of the family."

She was also the woman Zain had visited a few weeks ago, and darn if she wasn't gorgeous. "Where's Zain?" she asked, not caring if she hadn't used the proper address.

"He left and took the goons with him after I told him I couldn't do a proper examination with an audience."

Why not? She'd done a swan dive in front of one. "Any idea what happened to me, Dr. Barad?"

"You fainted. And please, call me Maysa." She pressed the metal cylinder against Madison's chest, listened for a few minutes and then pulled the stems from her ears. "It's definitely not your heart."

She wouldn't be surprised if it was, considering it was close to shattering. "That's good to know."

"Your blood pressure's stable, as well. I took it when you were passed out."

"Just wish I knew why I passed out."

"Are you eating well and getting enough rest?"

She'd been eating like a pig at a trough. "Yes on the eating, not so much on the rest. It's been fairly stressful around here." She didn't dare mention that Zain had been the primary cause of her lack of sleep.

Maysa dropped the stethoscope back in the bag and sent her a serious look. "When was your last menstrual cycle?"

An odd question since she'd never passed out from a period. "Honestly, I'm not sure, because they're not regular. I was born with only one ovary, and my doctor isn't convinced it functions all that well."

"Then you've been diagnosed as infertile?"

This was the complicated part. "Not exactly. I have been told that my chances of getting pregnant without medical assistance are remote and, even then, not guaranteed."

"How long ago was this?"

Madison had to think hard on that one, when all she wanted to do was go back to sleep. "I had an ultrasound ten years ago, but I always go for my annual checkups."

"Then you have no way of knowing for certain if perhaps your ovary is in fact functioning."

"I suppose that's accurate."

"Have your breasts been tender?"

Come to think of it, they had. Then again, they were Zain's favorite toys of late. "Maybe a little, but they get that way right before my period."

"That leads to my next question. Have you had sexual relations in the past month?"

She'd had sexual relations in the past few hours. "Why is that important?"

"Because your symptoms indicate you could be pregnant, provided you have been exposed."

Had she ever, and often. But pregnant? No way. "I'm really not sure how to answer that."

Maysa laid a gentle hand on her arm. "I promise you that anything you tell me will be held in the strictest of confidence. We also adhere to doctor-patient privilege in this country."

As long Madison didn't have to reveal who she'd been having relations with, she might as well admit it. "Yes, I have been exposed, but I truly can't imagine that I could be pregnant."

"There is one way to find out," she said. "I'll have a pregnancy test sent over in the morning."

Madison felt another faint coming on. "Can you make sure to be discreet?"

"I will." Maysa rose from the sofa and smiled down on her. "In the meantime, I want you to rest here awhile longer, and then retire to your room for the remainder of the evening. If you have any more spells, don't hesitate to have Zain call me."

She mentally nixed that suggestion. "Thank you. I appreciate that."

"Also, even if the test is negative, you should stop by my office and I'll draw some blood to be more certain. It could be you've eaten some tainted food."

Lovely. She hated needles about as much as she hated being viewed as fragile. "I'll let you know as soon as I know."

Maysa reached the door, paused with her hand on the knob and then faced Madison again. "You might want to forewarn the father."

She couldn't even consider telling Zain now. "Believe me, he wouldn't want to be bothered."

Maysa sent her a knowing smile. "He might surprise you."

With that, the doctor left, and Madison tipped her head back on the sofa and stared at the ornate chandelier on the ceiling. She never dreamed she would prefer food poisoning over pregnancy, but considering the poor timing, and the circumstance, a baby was the last thing she needed. Definitely the last thing Zain needed.

Of course, she was leaping to large conclusions without good cause. She'd had unprotected sex with Jay for five years, and that had never resulted in a bun in her oven. Of course, Jay hadn't owned a magic fertility mountain, either.

Ridiculous. All of it. She didn't know why she'd fainted, but she highly doubted pregnancy had anything to do with it.

The day had started off like any other day. Madison had awakened that morning after sleeping almost sixteen hours straight, taken a shower, picked out her clothes—and peed on a stick. Now it had suddenly become a day like no other.

She stared at the positive results for a good ten minutes before it finally began to sink in. She was going to have a baby. Zain's baby. A baby she'd always secretly wanted but convinced herself she would never have.

Myriad thoughts swarmed in her head, followed by one important question. How was she going to tell Zain? More important, should she even tell Zain?

He did have a right to know, but he also had the upcoming coronation hanging over his head. He had an entire country counting on him, too. A country that had finally begun to accept him. A scandal—any scandal—could ruin everything.

Right then she wanted to crawl back under the covers and cry the day away, as well as weigh her options. But when someone knocked on the door, and if it happened to be Zain, she might be forced to make a snap decision.

She tightened the sash on her robe, secured her damp hair at her nape, convened her courage and opened the door.

"Good morning, *cara,*" Elena said as she breezed into the room, a tray in her hands and something white tucked beneath her arm.

After taking one whiff of the food, Madison began to feel queasy. "Thanks, but my appetite isn't up to par."

Elena faced her with concern. "Are you still not feeling well?"

She dropped down on the edge of the bed. "I'm still a little weak."

"Then I will give strict orders you are not to be disturbed. But you need to eat something to regain your strength. Perhaps I should bring you some tea."

"No," she belted out. "I mean, schnapps probably wouldn't be good for an upset stomach." Definitely not good for a developing baby.

"I would bring you ginger tea to help with the nausea." She removed the cloth from beneath her arm and held it up. "I have also brought you fresh towels should you decided to take a long bath later."

"I appreciate that," she said, before it suddenly dawned on her Elena was heading into the bathroom, and the blasted test was still on the counter.

She could try to distract her. She could tackle her. Or she could accept that it was already too late, because the minute Elena came back into the room, she could tell the secret was out by the look on the woman's face.

"I see you have confirmed you are with child," Elena said in a remarkable matter-of-fact tone.

"Looks to be that way, but it's possible to have a false positive reading." Her last hope, and a remote one at that.

Elena looked altogether skeptical. "It is possible, but not probable when a Mehdi and a mountain are involved."

She'd drink to that, if she could drink. "You're making a huge assumption. How do you know I didn't have a torrid night with the chef?" *Dumb, Madison, really dumb.*

"The chef is nearing seventy years of age, and he can barely stand. I also knew from the beginning you would not be able to resist Prince Zain, and he would not be able to resist you."

Madison couldn't prevent the waterworks from turning on again. "I swear I never meant for this to happen," she said as she furiously swiped at the tears. "I have never crossed professional lines and I have never been so weak. I also never believed I'd be able to conceive a child."

Elena perched on the edge of the bed and took her hand. "You have never met a man like Prince Zain."

That wasn't even up for debate. "He is one in a million. An enigma and complex and very persuasive."

"He is his father in that respect."

Madison had the strongest feeling there could be a personal story behind that comment. She didn't have the strength to delve into more high drama. "And tomorrow, he's going to replace his father. He doesn't need this complication."

"He does need to see that you are all right. He has been so consumed with that need, he has taken to ordering everyone around like a petulant child."

That was news to her. She figured he'd gotten so caught up in the precoronation activities, she'd been the last thing on his mind. "Then why hasn't he stopped by?"

"Because Dr. Barad ordered him to stay away from you for at least twenty-four hours."

She experienced a measure of satisfaction that he was concerned, but she also feared his reaction when she lowered the baby boom. If she decided to make the revelation.

"Have you given any thought to when you are going to tell him?" Elena asked, as if she'd channeled her concerns.

That's all she'd been thinking about. "I have no idea.

I'm not even sure I should tell him." She held her breath and waited for a lecture on the virtues of honesty.

"Some would say it would be wrong to withhold such important information from Prince Zain," Elena began. "But I know the seriousness of the people's expectations when it comes to their ruler. You could be viewed as an outsider and unworthy of the king. You could be shunned, and so could your child. And Prince Zain's standing could forever be tarnished beyond repair."

She knew all those things, but that didn't make it easier to hear them. "And that's my dilemma, Elena. I wish I were better emotionally equipped to handle it, but I'm not. I'm worried that if I do tell him, he'll be angry and he'll send me immediately packing." That would solve her problem, but it would hurt to the core.

Elena squeezed her hand. "When the rumors surfaced about the paternity issues involving the Prince Zain and the model, I knew they were not true. He would never abandon his child, nor would he abandon the woman he loves with all his heart."

"He's never said he loves me, Elena." But then she had never told him, either.

"He is like any other man, afraid to say the word for fear he will swallow his tongue and never speak again, among other things."

They shared in a brief laugh before the seriousness of the situation settled over Madison again. "If what you say is true, then I would be asking him to choose between me and his child, and his country. And if he does choose us, he might regret that decision the rest of his life, and in turn resent me."

"That is possible."

Madison fought back another onslaught of tears. "Please tell me what to do, Elena."

"Only you can decide, *cara*. And you must ask yourself two important questions. Are you strong enough to stay, if that is what he wants from you, and do you love him enough to let him go if you decide not to ask that of him?"

She did love him enough to choose the latter. She couldn't ask him to choose and risk he'd hate her for it. She'd rather part as friends, and live on a lifetime of memories. As far as what she would tell their child, she'd have to figure that out later when she had a clearer head and a less heavy heart.

Elena brushed a kiss across Madison's cheek before she stood. "Whatever you decide, please know I believe you are more than worthy of Prince Zain's love. If the situation were different, I would welcome you as the daughter I was never fortunate enough to have."

Madison came to her feet and gave her a long hug. "And I would be proud to be your daughter-in-law, Elena." If things were different, which they weren't. "I can't thank you enough for you advice and support."

"You are welcome, *cara*," she said with a kind smile. "And should you be in need of a governess after the baby's birth, please keep me in mind. I would be happy to raise another Mehdi son or daughter."

She appreciated the offer, though she couldn't imagine Elena ever leaving this place. "I will definitely keep it in mind."

"And I will be praying for a bright and happy future for you both."

After Madison saw Elena out, it became all too clear what she had to do. She crossed the room, picked up the phone and pounded out Deeb's extension. When he answered with his usual dry greeting, she dispensed with all pleasantries. "This is Madison Foster. Could you please reschedule my flight for first thing in the morning?"

A span of silence passed before he responded. "You do not wish to attend the coronation?"

She couldn't very well tell the truth, so she handed him a partial lie. "I'm really disappointed I can't attend, but I have a job offer and they want me to start immediately."

"Should I inform the emir you've had a change in plans?"

"No. I'll tell him." Or not.

"As you wish."

After she hung up, Madison curled up on the bed to take another nap. She needed more rest to regain her strength before she took the last step. A step that she didn't want to take—the final goodbye to the man she loved.

When Zain opened the door and saw the sadness in Madison's eyes, he knew why she had arrived unexpectedly in his quarters. She was not there only to wish him well, though she probably would. She was not there to spend one final night in his arms, though he wished she would. She was there to say her goodbyes.

"May I come in?" she asked, sounding unsure and unhappy.

He opened the door wide. "Please do."

Once inside, they fell into an uncomfortable silence before she spoke again. "I went by your office first but Mr. Deeb said you'd retired early, so that's why I'm here. I hope it's okay."

"Of course. You have been here before."

"I know, but never through the front door."

That brought about both their smiles, yet hers faded

fast. "Come and sit with me awhile." *Stay with me for-ever.* The thought arrived with the force of a grenade. A wish he could not fulfill.

After he cleared several documents from the sofa, Madison took a seat on the end, while he claimed the chair across from her. "You look much better than you did the last time I saw you. Are you feeling better?"

"Much better. I've had plenty of sleep."

He could not say the same for himself. "Did Maysa determine why you fainted?"

"It could be a number of things, but all that matters now is I'm fine."

She sounded less than confident, and that concerned him. "I am happy to hear that. I've been very worried about you since I had to catch you during your fall."

"You caught me?" She both sounded and looked taken aback.

"I would never let you fall, Madison." And he would never forget those moments of intense fear. "Do you not remember?"

She shook her head. "No. I just remember being dizzy, and then I woke up on the couch."

"I was furious when Maysa demanded I leave you alone." He still was.

"Elena told me you were not in the best of moods. I'm sure my little mishap, coupled with the upcoming cere-mony, didn't help. So are you nervous about tomorrow?"

No, but she was. He could tell by the way she folded the hem of her causal blue top back and forth. "I am ready for it to be over." Though that meant they would be over, as well.

"I'm sure you are. But it's the realization of your dreams, and that has to make you happy."

Holding her would make him happy. Having her as a

part of that dream would be the ultimate happiness. He felt he could do neither. "You should be happy to witness the fruits of your labor when I am officially crowned."

Her gaze faltered. "I didn't do that much, Zain."

He would strongly disagree. "You managed to mold me into the king I was meant to be, and that was no small accomplishment." She'd managed to steal his heart in the process.

She presented a sincere smile. "Yeah, you were a challenge at times. But I wouldn't take a moment of it back."

Nor would he, and he could not let another minute pass without being closer to her. He pushed off the chair and joined her on the sofa, much to her apparent dismay when she slid over as far as she could go.

"You need not be concerned," he said. "I am not going to touch you unless you want me to do so."

She sighed. "I would love for you to touch me, but that would only make it harder to leave you tonight."

He took a chance and clasped her hand. "Then stay with me tonight. Better still, stay with me after the coronation."

She pulled her hand from his grasp. "And what would my duties be, Zain? Your staff consultant, or your staff mistress?"

He experienced the resurgence of the anger he had harbored all day. "I am not my father. I have never viewed you as my mistress."

"But that's exactly what I would be when you choose your proper royal wife. Of course, you could send me on my way when that happens. And that would probably be best since I couldn't stand the thought of some other woman in your bed."

He could not stand the thought of any other woman in his bed aside from her. "I wish I could promise we could have an open relationship, but that is not possible. We would both suffer for it."

"Then I guess we will just have to suffer through a permanent goodbye."

When she came to her feet, Zain stood, as well. "I am asking you not to go, Madison. I am begging you to stay."

She lowered her eyes. "What would be the point?"

He framed her face in his palms, forcing her to look at him. "Because I care for you, and I want your smile to be my last memory before you leave."

When she laid her hands on his, he expected her to wrench them away. Fortunately, she did not. "If you really cared about me, you wouldn't do this. You'd realize this is tearing me up inside."

"And you would realize it is killing me to say goodbye tonight. I promise I only want to hold you, and to know you are beside me in the morning on the most important day of my life."

"You are asking so much from me, Zain. Too much from us."

Desperation drove him to continue to plead his case. "I am asking you to give us this final night together."

"But I'm not strong around you."

When he saw the first sign of tears in her eyes, he tipped his forehead against hers. "You are strong, Madison, and you have given me strength when I have needed it most." He pulled back and thumbed away the moisture from her cheek. "You said you trusted me before. Trust me now."

"I'd keep you awake with my crying."

"I will gladly provide my shoulder."

He seemed to wait an eternity for her to speak again. "Do you promise not to steal the covers?"

His spirits rose at the sight of her smile. "I promise I will do my best."

"Then I'll stay." She pointed at him. "You have to wear clothes, and you can't try to seduce me."

He held the power to do that, but her faith in him was paramount. "I will remain dressed, and I will be on my best behavior." While battling the clothing constraints and his ever-present desire for her.

"Okay." She hid a yawn behind her hand. "Then let's get on with it before I pass out again."

His worry returned. "Do you feel that you might faint?"

"No, but I might fall asleep on my feet."

As she entered the bathroom, Zain retrieved a pair of unused pajama bottoms from the bureau and ignored the top. He had promised he would remain dressed, but he hadn't said how dressed he would be.

In an effort to hide his bare chest, he climbed into bed, pushed the wall switch that controlled the overhead light and covered up to his chin. She soon emerged from the bath and snapped on the nightstand lamp to reveal she was wearing one of his shirts. Clearly she meant to torture him.

She stood by the bed, a hand on her hip and a frown on her face. "Are you wearing anything, or have you already gone back on your word?"

He reluctantly lifted the sheet. "I am covered from the waist down and I feel that is a good compromise. You know I tend to get warm at night."

"Fine. Scoot over."

After he complied, Madison slid onto the mattress and snapped off the light. When she remained on her side, away from him, normally he would fit himself to her back. Tonight, he felt compelled to ask her permission. "May I hold you?"

"Yes, you may," she answered without looking at him.

He settled against her, slipped one arm beneath her and draped the other over her hip. The scent of her hair, the warmth of her body, sent him into immediate turmoil. After a while, when he heard the sound of her steady breathing, he began to relax. Knowing she was there with him, if only for tonight, provided the comfort he needed. His eyes grew heavy and he soon drifted off.

He had no idea how long he had been asleep when he was awakened by the feel of Madison's soft lips on his neck.

Not knowing if her affection stemmed from a dream, Zain remained frozen from fear of making the wrong move. But when she whispered, "One more memory," he knew she was fully awake.

She was already undressed, and she made sure he joined her in short order. With nothing between them but bare skin, they kissed for long moments, touched with abandon. And when those kisses and touches led to the natural conclusion, Madison took the lead, and he let her. She straddled his hips, rose above him and guided him inside her.

Zain acknowledged this was her means to maintain some control, by leading him into the depths of pleasure, and he gladly followed. He watched her face as she found her climax, and realized he had never seen her look so beautiful. Yet his own body demanded release, and it came, hard and fast.

When Madison stretched out on top of him, their bodies still joined, he rubbed her back gently. He had never felt so deeply for anyone, and he had never cherished her enough until that moment, knowing that she had given him this final, lasting gift of lovemaking. He wished they could suspend time and remain this way indefinitely, but that was impossible.

He refused to consider that now. Refused to take away from this time with her. And when he felt her tears dampen his shoulder, he held her closer and wished he could do more. If wishes were coins, he'd have enough to fill the entire palace. Yet he would never be able to fill the empty place in his soul when she left him. At least he would have some time with her tomorrow, and that thought helped him sleep.

Zain was sound asleep when Madison left his bed right before dawn. She hated to depart without his knowledge, but she didn't want to wake him. She was afraid to wake him. Afraid because he could easily persuade her back into bed and back into his arms. Maybe even persuade her to stay for the coronation, and even longer.

As it stood now, she had a plane to catch at the airstrip in an hour, a car coming in twenty minutes before that, and she still had to take a shower and finish packing. She hurriedly re-dressed in the bathroom, and when she returned to the bedroom, she thankfully found Zain sleeping like a baby.

A baby...

She couldn't think about that now or she'd start crying again, even though she felt all cried out. But she wasn't stupid enough to believe there wouldn't be more tears in her future. A lot of tears, along with a bucketful of regrets. Regret that he couldn't be a part of their child's life. Her life.

Madison took a chance and quietly approached the bed even though she risked waking Zain, but she couldn't leave just yet. The first signs of daylight allowed her to take a mental snapshot of him to help her remember these last moments. He looked almost innocent with that dark lock of hair falling over his forehead. And because he was stretched out on his belly, with his head toward her on the pillow, she could see his eyes move behind closed lids. He was probably dreaming about becoming king, but to her he would always be a desert knight with a winning smile and a hero's heart. Maybe he hadn't rescued her, but he had given her the most precious of gifts.

On that thought, she lifted his arm that was draped over the side of the mattress, and pressed his hand lightly against the place where their baby grew inside her. Someday, when their child's questions about his or her father inevitably began to come, she would simply say *Daddy loves you,* because she inherently knew he would.

As the tears began to threaten, and Zain slightly stirred, she released his hand and placed it on the empty space she had occupied so many nights. Then she leaned down and kissed his cheek. "Good night, sweet prince. I love you."

She walked away, praying she didn't hear him calling her name. But she heard only silence as she left his room for the last time. She experienced relief knowing she could leave before he even realized she was gone.

Ten

"What do you mean she is gone?"

Zain could swear Deeb physically flinched, the first sign of a crack in his unyielding demeanor. "She called yesterday evening and asked me to arrange for her flight to be moved to this morning."

He'd mistakenly believed that when he awoke to the empty space in his bed, she had left to dress for the coronation. "Did she say why she needed to depart early?"

"She mentioned something about a job offer that required her immediate return to the States."

Madison had never mentioned that to him. In fact, she had led him to believe she would be in attendance at his crowning. He wondered what other lies she had told him.

Driven by fury, he grabbed the ceremonial robe from the hanger behind his desk, slipped it on and began buttoning it with a vengeance. "If that is all, you may go."

"Prince Rafiq requests a meeting with you before the ceremony."

His brother should be on his honeymoon, not hovering like a vulture. "Tell him to meet me here in ten minutes, and I will allow him five."

Deeb bowed. "Yes, Your Majesty."

"Will you allow your former governess some of your precious time?"

At the sound of the endearing voice, Zain looked across the room to see Elena standing in the doorway, dressed in her finest clothes, her silver hair styled into a neat twist. "You may come in and stay as long as you wish."

She swept into the room and gave Deeb a smirk as she passed by him. After Zain took a seat behind his desk, Elena claimed the opposing chair. She folded her hands in her lap and favored him with a motherly smile. "I do not have to tell you how proud I am of your accomplishments."

The anger returned with ten times the force. "At least I have your support. Unfortunately, I cannot say the same for Madison, who took it upon herself to leave without telling me."

Elena practically sneered at him. "Remove your *testa* from your *culo*. You have no one to blame but yourself for her actions."

He did not appreciate being blamed for something beyond his control, especially by the one woman he could always count on. "I did not tell her to leave early."

"But did you ask her stay, *caro?*"

He forked both hands through his hair before folding them atop the desk. "I did, yet she refused me."

"How did you ask her?"

"I requested she stay on after the coronation, and then she accused me of asking her to be her mistress."

"If your request was not accompanied by a marriage proposal, then she was justified in her accusation."

He had no patience left for her lecture. "She knows that marriage between us is not possible. There would be severe repercussions."

"Then you are saying you would marry her if the situation were different?"

He did not know what he was saying at this point in time. He only knew he had already begun to miss her, and she was barely gone. "I see no need to speculate on impossibilities."

She leaned forward, reached across the desk and took his hands. "You must ask yourself now if sacrificing love for the sake of duty will be worth it."

"I have never claimed to love her."

"Then tell me now you do not."

If he did, he would be lying. He chose to cite a truth. "I am committed to ruling this country, as it has been ordained by the king."

She let go of his hands, leaned back and laughed. "*Caro,* you never cared about your father's wishes before. You must assume this responsibility because it is right for you, not because he challenged you or because he issued a royal command in an attempt to keep you reined in."

"Do you truly believe that was the intent?"

"Yes, I do. He saw so much of your mother in you. She was also a free spirit and fiercely independent. Since he could not control her, he was determined to keep you under his thumb by making unreasonable demands."

He had never heard her mention his mother in those terms. "I assumed he believed I was the most suitable son to answer the challenge. I should not be surprised he had other motivations, or that he never believed in me."

"He was somewhat calculating, Zain, but he was not a stupid man. He would never have designated you as his successor if he did not think you up to the challenge. And I personally believe you would make a magnificent king, but the demands could suffocate you in the process. I do not want you to live your life regretting what might have been had you chosen a different path."

He felt as though he were suffocating now. "Then I shall prove you both wrong."

Rafiq entered the room, a folder beneath his arm and a solemn expression on his face. He leaned down and kissed Elena's cheek. "The ceremony is set to begin. I have reserved a seat in the front row for you."

She smiled up at him. "Thank you, *caro mio*. And I want you to know that I believe you would make a good king, as well."

Elena quickly rose from the chair and leveled her gaze on Zain. *"Il vero amore e senza rimpianti."*

Real love is without regret....

The words echoed in Zain's mind as Rafiq pulled up the chair where Elena had been seated. "What was that all about?" he asked.

"Nothing." He had no reason to offer a valid explanation for something Rafiq would not understand. He did have a pressing question to pose. "Were you aware of Ms. Foster's early departure?"

Rafiq opened the notebook and studied the page. "No, but her absence is favorable today. You do not need any distractions."

Zain could argue she meant much more to him than a distraction, but he would only be met with cynicism. "How is Rima?"

"She is well," he said without looking up.

"Is she not disappointed that you are here and not on a wedding trip?"

Again, Rafiq failed to tear his attention away from the documents. "My wife understands the importance of my duties, and today my duty is to see that the transition goes smoothly." He finally looked up. "You have a full schedule. The press conference begins immediately following the ceremony, then you will be expected to attend a luncheon with several of the region's emissaries. This evening, you have the official gala."

He would rather eat lye than spend an evening suffering through another barrage of sultans attempting to foist their daughters off on him. "How many people will be in attendance?"

He closed the notebook. "Several hundred. I have to commend Ms. Foster on her assistance with the attendees. She somehow arranged for the U.S. vice president to be there, along with the British prime minister."

"She did not mention that to me."

"She wanted to surprise you."

Zain was surprised to learn the news, but not surprised she pulled it off. He checked his watch to see that he had little time before the ceremony, and found his thoughts turning to Madison. He wondered where she was at this moment, if she happened to be remembering their night together, or attempting to forget him. Perhaps he would call her later, or perhaps not. After today, he could offer her nothing more than a conversation that could cause them only longing, and pain.

He rose from the chair, removed the royal blue sash from the box on the corner of his desk—the sash that his father and his father's father had worn during their reign—and placed it around his neck. "I am ready now." Was he ready? He had no choice but to be ready.

"Before you go," Rafiq began, "I want you to know that although we do not always see eye to eye, I am proud of your accomplishments thus far, particularly your water conservation plans. I have lobbied the council members and I am happy to report all but one are now on board."

"Who is the holdout?"

"Shamil, and that is because I have not been able to reach him since my wedding that he did not bother to attend."

Zain found that odd since Shamil had been Rafiq's closest friend, the reason why Shamil had been appointed to the council. "Perhaps he is traveling."

"Perhaps, but that is not a concern at the moment. Let us away before we are late."

As Zain walked the corridor leading to the ceremonial chamber, with Deeb and Rafiq falling behind him, each step he took filled him with dread. Not dread over assuming the responsibility, but dread over making a mistake he could not take back. When they passed the area lined with attendees held back by braided gold ropes, he could only see visions of Madison. The remembrance of Elena's parting words overrode the burst of applause.

Il vero amore e senza rimpianti...real love is without regret.

And when the doors opened wide, revealing those who had received a special invitation to witness the ceremony, he stopped in his tracks.

"What are you waiting for, brother?"

Zain had been waiting all his life not for this moment, but for a woman like Madison Foster. Nothing else mattered—not his birthright, not duty, only his love for her. He would live with constant regret if he did not at least try to win her back, and that was much worse than the fallout from his next decision.

He turned to Rafiq, slipped the sash from his neck, and placed it around his brother's. "The crown is yours, Rafiq, as it should have been from the beginning. Wear it well."

Confusion crossed Rafiq's expression. "Are you saying—"

"I am abdicating."

"Why?"

"If I told you, you would not understand. Suffice it to say that I have learned commitment must come from the heart. Though I will remain committed to my country and intend to see my conservation plans implemented, my true commitment lies elsewhere."

Rafiq scowled. "You would give up your duty for a woman?"

"I am giving up my duty for love."

"Love is inconstant, Zain. It drives men to weakness."

"You are wrong, brother. It drives men to honor." Zain laid a hand on Rafiq's shoulder. "I am sorry you are so trapped in your love of duty that you will never know real love."

With that, he turned on his heels and left, ignoring the silent, esteemed guests who apparently had been rendered mute from shock.

When he reached the study, he stripped out of the robe, tossed it aside and began to mentally formulate a plan.

"Is there anything I can assist you with, Emir?"

He should have expected Deeb to come to his aid, as the faithful assistant had for years. "Call the airstrip and tell them to ready the second plane for immediate departure. After that, ask one of the staff to pack my bags."

Deeb moved into the room and stood at attention. "Where will you be going and for what length of time?"

He unlocked the drawer containing his passport. "I will be going to Washington, D.C., for an indeterminable about of time." He would only be there a matter of hours if Madison tossed him out on his *culo*.

"If you are going after Ms. Foster, she has not yet departed."

Zain's gaze snapped from the folder to Deeb. "Why is it that you are only now telling me this?"

"I assumed the plane would have taken off by now. It seems the pilot has delayed the flight due to inclement weather."

Zain peered out the window and as predicted, the sun was shining. "The rain stopped hours ago."

"Yes, Emir, it did," Deeb said.

The pilot must be an imbecile, or overly cautious, but either way, Zain was pleased. "Call the airfield and make certain the plane remains as it is."

"As you wish, Emir. Shall I accompany you?"

Zain pocketed the passport, rounded the desk and placed his hands on Deeb's shoulders. "No. You shall go home to your wife and children and spend a lengthy sabbatical in their company. I will make certain you are paid your wages until you resume your duties as my brother's assistant."

Deeb smiled, taking Zain by surprise. "I truly appreciate your consideration, Emir, and I hope that we meet again soon."

Perhaps sooner than he would like if he did not hurry. "Now that we have finalized my arrangements, I am off to see a woman about my future."

Delays, delays and more delays.

Madison leaned back in the leather seat and muttered a few mild oaths aimed at the idiot responsible for the three-hour wait on the tarmac. Unfortunately, she had no idea who that idiot might be, since she couldn't understand a word of the offered explanations.

But she couldn't complain about the service she'd received in the interim. She been plied with food and drink and even shown the onboard bed by the flight attendant. She preferred to nap in the seat, belted in, until they were safely in the air, hopefully by next week.

She checked her watch for the hundredth time and confirmed the ceremony should be over by now. Zain was probably being presented to the press as the newly crowned king of Bajul. She was happy that he had finally realized his dream, and sad that she couldn't play a part in it. Even sadder that he wouldn't be a part of his child's life.

When someone knocked on the exterior door at the front of the plane, Madison hoped someone had arrived either to inform them of takeoff, or to explain why they couldn't seem to get airborne. She watched as the attendant pulled down the latch, and then the woman bowed. Madison wondered if some dignitary had delayed the flight in order to hitch a ride. If so, she hoped he or she didn't expect a friendly reception from her.

But when she saw the tall, gorgeous guy step into the aisle, she realized she'd been wrong—very wrong.

As if he didn't have a care in the world, Zain flipped his sunglasses up on his head and dropped down in the seat beside her.

"What are you doing here?" she asked around her astonishment.

He presented a world-class grin. "I've decided you could use some company on your journey."

He had lost his ever-lovin' royal mind. "You can't do that. You just became king. They're not going to tolerate you running out on your obligations on a whim."

He lifted her hand and laced their fingers together. "This is not a whim. This is a plea for your forgiveness."

"I forgive you," she said. "Now leave before they oust you from the palace on your royal behind and strip you of your crown."

"They cannot do that."

"Maybe not, but since you've worked so hard to restore your reputation as a non-flight risk, don't you think it would be beneficial to actually prove that is the case?"

"My reputation is no longer a concern."

Had she taught him nothing? "It should be, Zain, if you're going to be an effective king."

"I am not the king."

Her mouth momentarily opened before she snapped it shut. "If you're not the king, then who is?"

"I abdicated to Rafiq."

She took a moment to sort through the questions running through her brain at breakneck speed. "Why would you do that when this has been your dream forever?"

He brushed a kiss across her cheek. "It was my father's dream, or perhaps I should say his ploy to keep me under his control, according to Elena, who told me that this morning. Being with you is my real dream, although I did not know that until I was faced with what I stood to lose if I lost you."

Alarm bells rang out in Madison's head. "What else did Elena tell you?"

"She told me that if I chose the crown over you, I would only live with regret, and she was correct. I want to be with you as long as you will have me."

She was still stuck on his conversation with Elena. "And that's all she said?"

He frowned. "Should there be more?"

"I guess not." She felt relieved that he appeared to be

in the dark about the pregnancy, and thrilled that he had returned to her without that knowledge. But still… "I'm worried you're going to regret this decision to give up everything you've worked for and what you still have left to achieve. Not when you've made it so clear how much you love your country."

"I love you more."

She couldn't quite believe her ears. "What did you say?"

"I said I love you more than my country. More than my wealth and more than my freedom."

After his declaration began to sink in, Madison said the only thing she could think to say. "I love you, too."

He gave her the softest, most genuine smile. "Enough to marry me?"

Not once had she let herself imagine that question. "Zain, we haven't known each other that long. In fact, we've never really dated. Maybe we should just start there."

He lifted her hand for a kiss. "A wise woman recently told me that an immediate connection to a person leaves a lasting impact."

"Elena's words?"

"No. Maysa's. She told me that when I talked nonstop about you the night I went to see her. And she is right. I have felt connected to you since the day we met, and I want to make that connection legal and legitimate in everyone's eyes."

If he was willing to take that leap of faith, why wouldn't she jump, too? After all, they had a child to consider—information she needed to reveal, and soon. But before she could force the words out of her mouth, the door to the cockpit opened, and in walked none other than Adan, wearing his military flight suit and his trademark dimpled grin.

Zain shot out of his seat and moved into the aisle. "What are you doing here?"

Adan responded with a grin. "I am flying the plane, of course, and you should thank me. I'm the reason why we have yet to take off."

"I do not understand, Adan."

Neither did Madison, but she couldn't wait to hear the youngest Mehdi's explanation.

"I delayed our departure because I suspected you would come to your senses and realize you could not let a woman like Madison leave."

"You came upon that conclusion on your own?" Zain asked in a suspicious tone.

Adan looked a little sheepish. "All right, I admit that Elena formulated the plan, and I agreed to it. And if it had not worked, I planned to whisk Madison to Paris, which by the way is where we will be stopping for the night to refuel."

"You have a woman waiting for you there," Zain said.

Adan grinned again. "That is a distinct possibility."

Zain pointed to the cockpit. "Fly the plane."

"That is my plan, brother. And feel free to utilize the onboard bed during our flight."

"The plane," Zain repeated.

After Adan retreated, Zain returned to Madison and clasped her hand once more. "Let's marry in Paris."

Oh, how she wanted to say yes. But first, she had a serious revelation to make. "Before I agree to marriage, there's something I need to tell you."

"You are not already married, are you?"

She smiled. "No, but I am pregnant."

He stared at her for a moment before comprehension dawned in his stunned expression. "You are serious?"

"Yes, I am serious. I wouldn't joke about a thing like that." But she wasn't beyond using humor to defuse his possible anger over the secret. "And that's the reason why I fainted. It wasn't bad food or your overwhelming charisma, although that does make me want to swoon now and then."

When he failed to immediately comment, Madison worried that her attempts at levity hadn't worked. That brought about her explanation as to why she had withheld the information. "I wanted to tell you, Zain, but I didn't want you to have to choose between the baby and your obligation to your country. And I also need you to understand that it's not that I didn't want a child, I just thought I could never have one. I never wanted to deceive you, but—"

He stopped her words with a kiss. "It's all right, Madison. I could not feel more blessed at this moment."

Neither could she. "Then you're okay with it?"

"I will be okay when you say that you will marry me."

Madison held her breath, and finally took that all-important leap. "Yes, I will marry you."

Any reservations or hesitation melted away with Zain's kiss. In a few months, she would finally have the baby she'd always wanted and thought she would never have, with the man she would always love.

Epilogue

"Here are your babies, Mrs. Mehdi."

After the nurse placed the bundles in the crooks of Madison's arms, she could only stare at her son and daughter in absolute awe. Not only had her lone ovary functioned well, it had worked double time. She only wished their father had been there to see them come into the world.

As if she'd willed his presence, Zain rushed into the room sporting a huge bouquet of red roses and an apologetic look. "The damn plane was delayed because of the rain," he said as he set the flowers down and stripped off his coat.

No surprise to Madison. Wherever there was rain, there was Zain. "It's okay, Daddy. Just get over here and see what you've done."

He slowed his steps on the way to the hospital bed, as if he were afraid to look. But when he took that first glance at his babies, his eyes reflected unmistakable joy, and so did his smile. "I cannot believe they are finally here."

Neither could Madison. "After fourteen hours of labor, I was beginning to wonder."

He leaned over to softly kiss her. "I regret I was not here with you to see you through this."

"That's okay. Elena stayed the entire time and held my hand, worrying like a mother hen."

"Where is she now?"

"I sent her back to the condo. She mentioned something about napping beneath the California sun so she could work on her tan."

He smiled as he brushed a fingertip across their daughter's cheek. "She is beautiful, like her mother."

Madison pushed the blanket away from their son's face to give his father a better look. "And our baby boy is so handsome, just like his uncle Adan."

That earned her a serious scowl. "You are determined to punish me for my late arrival."

"No, I'm just trying to cheer you up, but I guess under the circumstance, that's not going to be easy to do."

"No, it is not." He scooped their daughter into his arms with practiced ease, as if he'd been a father forever, not five minutes. "Holding new life in your arms helps ease the sadness."

It had definitely been a time of sadness back in Bajul, as well as a week full of unanswered questions. "How is Rafiq doing?"

"It is hard to tell," he said. "He seemed all right at the funeral, but he is not one to show any emotion."

Madison had learned that firsthand. During the the two times she and Zain had returned to Bajul, she couldn't recall seeing Rafiq smile all that much. Then, neither had his bride. "I wish I had known Rima better. Do they have any idea what happened with the car, or why she was even in it alone that time of night?"

When the baby began to fuss, Zain lifted their daughter to his shoulder. "No true explanations have emerged thus far. As it was with my mother's death, we may never know."

For months Madison had considered telling her husband about the conversation with Elena involving his mother, but she'd decided to put that on hold for the time being. Today should be about the joy of new beginnings, not sorrow and regrets.

The nurse returned to the room and when she caught sight of Zain, Madison thought the woman might collapse. It didn't matter if they were seventeen or seventy—and this woman was closer to the latter—females always responded the same way to Zain. "Is this the babies' daddy?" she asked.

No, he's the chauffeur, Madison wanted to say but bit back the sarcasm. "Ruth, this is my husband, Zain."

When Zain stood to shake her hand, Ruth grinned from ear to ear. "It's a pleasure to meet you. Is it true you're a sheikh?"

"Yes," Zain said. "But today I am only a new father."

Madison couldn't be more proud of that fact, or the way he pressed a soft kiss on his daughter's forehead. She was definitely going to be a daddy's girl.

The nurse lumbered over to the bed and took Madison's baby boy out of her arms, much to her dismay. "Where are you going with him?"

Ruth patted Madison's arm. "Don't worry, Mommy. He'll just be gone for a little while. Now that he and his sister have warmed up a bit, it's time for their first bath."

She was a little disappointed to give up her children

so soon after their birth, but it would allow her and Zain some time to reach one important decision.

After Ruth carted off the twins, Madison scooted over, gritted her teeth against the lingering pain of childbirth and patted the space beside her. "Come over here, you sexy sheikh."

He turned his smile on her. "Is it not too soon to consider that?"

She rolled her eyes. "I just gave birth to the equivalent of two five-pound bowling balls, so what do you think?"

"You have a point." He kicked off his Italian loafers, climbed onto the narrow bed and folded her into his arms.

"We need to decide on their names," she said as she rested her cheek against his chest. "We can't just refer to them as 'He' and 'She' Mehdi indefinitely, although it is kind of catchy."

"How do you feel about Cala for our daughter?" he asked.

Zain had never suggested that name before now, but Madison supposed his trip home to mourn after the end of a young woman and her unborn child's life had somehow influenced his choice. "It's perfect. I'm sure your mother would have loved having a granddaughter named after her."

"Then we shall call her that. And our son?"

She lifted her head and smiled. "Why not settle for what we've been calling him the past five months?" The nickname they'd given him the day they'd learned the babies' genders during the ultrasound.

He grinned. "Joe?"

"Short for Joseph, which just happens to be my great-great-grandfather's name."

"Joseph it is."

Now that they had covered that all-important decision, she needed to address one more. "Do you have any regrets about giving up the crown and leaving Bajul?"

"Only one. We never made love on the rooftop."

She elbowed his ribs. "I'm serious."

"I have a beautiful wife and two perfect children. How could I possibly regret that?" His expression turned somber. "Do you regret that you have put your career on hold for me?"

Something Madison had sworn she would never do, but then she's never imagined loving a man this much. And during the last conversation with her mother, she'd actually admitted it. "I haven't put my career completely on hold. I'll be doing some preliminary consulting for the senator's campaign the first of the year."

"And you do not mind traveling to Bajul in a few months and staying for a time?"

"As long as we wait until my parents come for their visit, I'm more than game. Besides, I've told you that I feel it's important that our children know their culture, and you still have important work to do on your conservation plans."

He planted a quick kiss on her lips. "Good. While we're there, we will return to the lake and relive our first experience."

The experience that had brought them to this day. This new life. This incredible love. "That sounds like a plan. You bring Malik's truck, and I'll bring my overactive ovary. We might even get lucky a second time."

"I cannot imagine feeling any luckier than I do now."

"Neither can I."

When the nurse returned their children to their waiting arms, completing the family they had made, Madison and Zain settled into comfortable silence, as they'd done so many times since they had taken that giant leap of faith, and landed in the middle of that sometimes treacherous territory known as love.

Madison felt truly blessed, and it was all because of one magical mountain, and one equally magical man. A man who might not be the king of his country, but he was—and always would be—the king of her heart.

* * * * *

#2233 SUNSET SEDUCTION
The Slades of Sunset Ranch
Charlene Sands

When the chance to jump into bed with longtime crush Lucas Slade comes along, Audrey Thomas can't help but seize it. Now the tricky part is to wrangle her way into the rich rancher's *heart*.

#2234 AFFAIRS OF STATE
Daughters of Power: The Capital
Jennifer Lewis

Can Ariella Winthrop—revealed as the secret love child of the U.S. president—find love with a royal prince whose family disapproves of her illegitimacy?

#2235 HIS FOR THE TAKING
Rich, Rugged Ranchers
Ann Major

It's been six years since Maddie Gray left town in disgrace. But now she's back, and wealthy rancher John Coleman can't stay away from the lover who once betrayed him.

#2236 TAMING THE LONE WOLFF
The Men of Wolff Mountain
Janice Maynard

Security expert Larkin Wolff lives by a code, but when he's hired to protect an innocent heiress, he's tempted to break all his rules and become *personally* involved with his client....

#2237 HOLLYWOOD HOUSE CALL
Jules Bennett

When an accident forces receptionist Callie Matthews to move in with her boss, her relationship with the sexy doctor becomes much less about business and *very* much about pleasure....

#2238 THE FIANCÉE CHARADE
The Pearl House
Fiona Brand

Faced with losing custody of her daughter, Gemma O'Neill will do anything—even pretend to be engaged to the man who fathered her child.

You can find more information on upcoming Harlequin®
titles, free excerpts and more at www.Harlequin.com.

HDCNM0513

REQUEST YOUR FREE BOOKS!
2 FREE NOVELS PLUS 2 FREE GIFTS!

◆ HARLEQUIN®

Desire

ALWAYS POWERFUL, PASSIONATE AND PROVOCATIVE

YES! Please send me 2 FREE Harlequin Desire® novels and my 2 FREE gifts (gifts are worth about $10). After receiving them, if I don't wish to receive any more books, I can return the shipping statement marked "cancel." If I don't cancel, I will receive 6 brand-new novels every month and be billed just $4.55 per book in the U.S. or $4.99 per book in Canada. That's a savings of at least 13% off the cover price! It's quite a bargain! Shipping and handling is just 50¢ per book in the U.S. and 75¢ per book in Canada.* I understand that accepting the 2 free books and gifts places me under no obligation to buy anything. I can always return a shipment and cancel at any time. Even if I never buy another book, the two free books and gifts are mine to keep forever.

225/326 HDN F4ZC

Name _____ (PLEASE PRINT) _____

Address _____ Apt. #

City _____ State/Prov. _____ Zip/Postal Code

Signature (if under 18, a parent or guardian must sign)

Mail to the **Harlequin® Reader Service:**
IN U.S.A.: P.O. Box 1867, Buffalo, NY 14240-1867
IN CANADA: P.O. Box 609, Fort Erie, Ontario L2A 5X3

Want to try two free books from another line?
Call 1-800-873-8635 or visit www.ReaderService.com.

* Terms and prices subject to change without notice. Prices do not include applicable taxes. Sales tax applicable in N.Y. Canadian residents will be charged applicable taxes. Offer not valid in Quebec. This offer is limited to one order per household. Not valid for current subscribers to Harlequin Desire books. All orders subject to credit approval. Credit or debit balances in a customer's account(s) may be offset by any other outstanding balance owed by or to the customer. Please allow 4 to 6 weeks for delivery. Offer available while quantities last.

Your Privacy—The Harlequin® Reader Service is committed to protecting your privacy. Our Privacy Policy is available online at www.ReaderService.com or upon request from the Harlequin Reader Service.

We make a portion of our mailing list available to reputable third parties that offer products we believe may interest you. If you prefer that we not exchange your name with third parties, or if you wish to clarify or modify your communication preferences, please visit us at www.ReaderService.com/consumerschoice or write to us at Harlequin Reader Service Preference Service, P.O. Box 9062, Buffalo, NY 14269. Include your complete name and address.

HD13R

SPECIAL EXCERPT FROM

presents

SUNSET SEDUCTION

The latest installment of USA TODAY *bestselling author*

Charlene Sands's miniseries

THE SLADES OF SUNSET RANCH

All grown up, Audrey Faith Thomas seizes her chance to act on a teenage crush. Now she must face the consequences....

U_{sually} not much unnerved Audrey Faith Thomas, except for the time when her big brother was bucked off Old Stormy at an Amarillo rodeo and broke his back.

Audrey shuddered at the memory and thanked the Almighty that Casey was alive and well and bossy as ever. But as she sat behind the wheel of her car, driving toward her fate, the fear coursing through her veins had nothing to do with her brother's disastrous five-second ride. This fear was much different. It made her want to turn her Chevy pickup truck around and go home to Reno and forget all about showing up at Sunset Ranch unannounced.

To face Lucas Slade.

The man she'd seduced and then abandoned in the middle of the night.

Audrey swallowed hard. She still couldn't believe what she'd done.

Last month, after an argument and a three week standoff with her brother, she'd ventured to his Lake Tahoe cabin to make amends. He'd been right about the boyfriend she'd just dumped and she'd needed Casey's strong shoulder to cry on.

The last person she'd expected to find there was Luke Slade—the man she'd measured every other man against—sleeping in the guest room bed, *her bed*. Luke was the guy she'd crushed on during her teen years while traveling the rodeo circuit with Casey.

Seeing him had sent all rational thoughts flying out the window. This was her chance. She wouldn't let her prudish upbringing interfere with what she needed. When he rasped, "Come closer," in the darkened room, she'd taken that as an invitation to climb into bed with him, consequences be damned.

Well…she'd gotten a lot more than a shoulder to cry on, and it had been glorious.

Now she would finally come face-to-face with Luke. She'd confront him about the night they'd shared and confess her love for him, if it came down to that. She wondered what he thought about her abandoning him that night.

She would soon find out.

Find out what happens when Audrey and Luke reunite in

SUNSET SEDUCTION
by Charlene Sands.

Available June 2013 from Harlequin® Desire®
wherever books are sold!